WAR ON THE HIGH SEAS

The gun crew, crouching with red bandanas knotted around their heads to save their eardrums from the cannon roar, saw the gunner captain chop down his arm and shout, "Fire, you bloody buggers! Fire!"

The burst from the *Eclipse*'s cannons was matched by a burst of flame from the pattimar's guns. Both vessels shuddered from the strikes.

Horne felt the deck tremble beneath his feet. He heard cries from amidship. The enemy had hit men, but he had no time to think about injuries or deaths. Deciding to change tack and fire on the enemy leeward, he halted when he saw the pattimar swing about, its snub nose turning towards the headland.

Horne raised his spyglass. Was the pattimar retreating?

The frigate's gun crew pulled off their bandanas and cheered as Lieutenant Pilkington rejoiced, "We bettered them, sir! We bettered them!"

Horne did not reply; he suspected the enemy had a plan of his own.

A call from the masthead confirmed his suspicions, "Sails ho! One to starboard! Second to larboard! Sails ho!"

Horne snapped open the spyglass. He spotted the first white speck moving from the headland. To his right he saw the tilting sail of another ship. Two more ships were joining the pattimar. The enemy had maneuvered the *Eclipse* into a trap. . . .

THE BOMBAY MARINES

An Adam Horne Adventure

Porter Hill

BERKLEY BOOKS, NEW YORK

Dedicated to the living spirit of Billie Ann.

This is a work of fiction. Names, characters, places, and incidents are either the product of the author's imagination or are used fictitiously, and any resemblance to actual persons, living or dead, business establishments, events, or locales is entirely coincidental.

THE BOMBAY MARINES

A Berkley Book / published by arrangement with
Walker Publishing Company, Inc.

PRINTING HISTORY
Walker Publishing Company, Inc. edition / September 1988
Berkley edition / November 2000

The Penguin Putnam Inc. World Wide Web site address is
http://www.penguinputnam.com

ISBN: 0-425-17786-6

BERKLEY®

Berkley Books are published by The Berkley Publishing Group,
a division of Penguin Putnam Inc.,
375 Hudson Street, New York, New York 10014.
BERKLEY and the "B" design
are trademarks belonging to Penguin Putnam Inc.

PRINTED IN THE UNITED STATES OF AMERICA

10 9 8 7 6 5 4 3 2 1

MAP OF INDIA c. 1761

PERSIA

MAKRAN COAST

RAJASTHAN   • Agra

• Hyderabad

BENGAL
Calcutta •

• Bombay

ARABIAN

SEA

N

LACCADIVE
ISLANDS

Fort St. George
Madras
Pondicherry •

BAY   OF

BENGAL

Chingleput Inlet

MALABAR COAST

Bull
Island

CEYLON

MALDIVE

ISLANDS

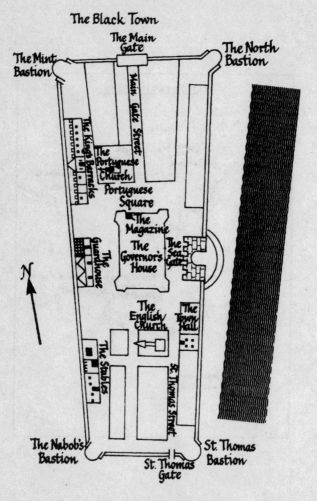

MAP OF FORT ST. GEORGE, MADRAS

The Black Town

The Mint Bastion

The Main Gate

The North Bastion

Main Gate Street

The King's Barracks

The Portuguese Church

Portuguese Square

The Magazine

The Guardhouse

The Governor's House

The Sea Gate

N

The English Church

The Town Hall

The Stables

St. Thomas Street

The Nabob's Bastion

St. Thomas Gate

St. Thomas Bastion

Shipyards

THE EAST INDIA COMPANY

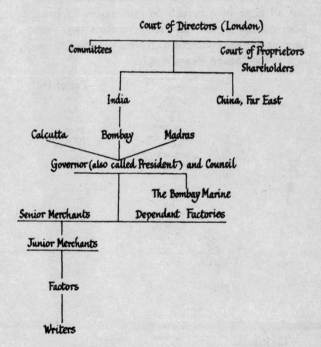

Court of Directors (London)

Committees   Court of Proprietors
Shareholders

India   China, Far East

Calcutta   Bombay   Madras

Governor (also called President) and Council

The Bombay Marine

Senior Merchants   Dependant Factories

Junior Merchants

Factors

Writers

Note

France's surrender of Pondicherry to England in 1761 lost all hope of a French colonial power in India. Both nations signed the Treaty of Paris two years later, ending the conflict which became known to history as the "Seven Years War."

—Porter Hill

PART ONE
Rough Orders

1

Bombay Castle

The south-easterly breeze off the Arabian Sea fluttered three flags run up high on the battlements of Bombay Castle. The first flag was England's Union Jack. The second was the red-and-white striped standard of the Honourable East India Company with the Union Jack squared in the upper left corner. The third flag was a duplicate of the East India Company's colours except for a dominant red cross making it as the ensign of the Company's private fighting unit—the Bombay Marine.

Captain Adam Horne paced a long hallway within the stone castle, his head bent forward, both hands gripped behind his back, waiting for an interview with Marine Commander-in-Chief, Commodore Watson.

Adam Horne had returned to Bombay less than twenty-four hours earlier. His frigate, the *Eclipse*, thirty-four guns, had been assigned to put an end to the Maratha pirates plaguing the East India Company's trading routes between Hyderabad and Persia. He carried a report of success in his pocket.

Horne's commission as captain was recent. The assignment to the North Arabian Sea had been his second appointment aboard the *Eclipse*. But today was the first time for him to submit a written report to the Commander-in-Chief.

Pacing the hallway, he wondered if he had written too much about his land attacks against Singee Ranjee's encampment. Would Commodore Watson be concerned with terrain details? Might a man with Watson's naval background prefer to be informed mostly about encounters at sea?

Reaching the end of the hallway, he raised his head and saw himself reflected in a tall, gilt-framed mirror. Leaning closer, he studied the creases forming around his eyes. He was not displeased by what he saw. Creases made him look older than his twenty-seven years, more mature than when he had left Bombay fourteen months ago, and a completely different person than the belligerent young man who had come out to India from England seven years ago, lonely, unhappy, looking for a new life.

Reaching up to his forehead, he tucked a tangle of chestnut hair under the front of the cocked hat. He believed that he looked more serious—less jaunty—when his hair did not tumble over his forehead. However, there was no way he could stop it curling in the sea air.

Adam Horne was a tall man, standing just over six feet. But he felt that his shoulders were too wide for the physical proportions of his angular body, giving him the look of a brute, and making him the first man a drunkard picked a fight with in a tavern. The passing years had taught him to accept such challenges less enthusiastically, sometimes even trying to discourage the fight.

Straightening his stance in front of the mirror, Horne's eyes dropped to the new dress uniform which had been tailored for him during his absence from Bombay, a coat and breeches that he wore for the first time today. What would a young lady make of him attired in this blue frock coat decorated with gold epaulettes and high-standing collar; the silk shirt with its long, winding stock; the pair of tied breeches and tall, black, horseleather boots? The East India Company had copied the uniform from His Majesty's Royal Navy. Horne suspected that a Marine officer's wife had been instrumental in the decision, some English woman who regretted that her husband was not in His Majesty's Forces and wanted him to look dashing despite the fact that he was attached to the badly disciplined, down-at-the-heel unit referred to with sniggers as the "Bombay Buccaneers."

Adjusting the gold and silver hilt of the sword hanging from his belt, Horne turned from the mirror, hoping that the East India Company did not have too many other changes planned for the Bombay Marine. If he had wanted an easy, dashing life, he would have joined one of the Forces considered to be gentlemanly and civilized, such as the Royal Navy, or the East India Company's Maritime Service which manned the Company's mammoth merchant ships. He resumed his pacing of the hallway, wondering about his future with the

Marine. Would he continue having the independence and freedom of manoeuvre he had had in his last assignment?

The Marine's primary function was to protect the Company's trading routes. But war raged with France, with the fighting now centralized on the opposite side of the Indian sub-continent from Bombay, and more than half of the Marine's nine frigates and ten peak-sailed gallivats had already been sent to join the Royal Navy in the Bay of Bengal. Horne feared that the *Eclipse* might suffer the same fate.

The click of a door latch attracted his attention. Turning, he saw Commodore Watson's secretary, Lieutenant Todwell, step out into the hallway.

"Captain Horne?"

"Lieutenant." Horne reached towards the sealed report bulging his pocket.

"Commodore Watson will see you now, Captain Horne."

Horne stepped in front of Lieutenant Todwell, nodding, fleetingly imagining the lean, sallow-cheeked secretary as a possible subordinate aboard the *Eclipse*. A shortage of manpower in the last fourteen months had taught him not to eliminate anyone as a potential recruit.

Commodore Watson, a big man with bushy eyebrows, fat jowls and a sunburnt nose, sat under the rattan sweeps of a *punkah* fan moving back and forth above his desk. Adam Horne's written report—its wax seal unbroken—lay amongst other official documents. Commodore Watson leaned back in his chair, dabbing a cotton square at the fleshy folds of his neck as he listened to Horne recounting the events of the last fourteen months. Occasionally he interrupted Horne to ask for details, information about land manoeuvres, how Horne had led his Marines against Singee Ranjee's mud fortress and strongholds in the Talari-Band Mountains. Watson grimaced when Horne told him about losing fourteen men in a late-night skirmish against a pirate camp east of Sonmiani Bay; he nodded approvingly when Horne explained that he had been forced to select men from the frigate's crew to supplement his Marine squadron; he smiled when Horne added that sailors made sad, clod-hopping Marines.

Raising one hand, he rasped in his hoarse, throaty voice, "Did lack of manpower hold you back, Horne?"

Horne considered the question. "I believe, sir, I would have suffered fewer casualties with more fighting men."

"But you accomplished your mission?"

"Yes, sir."

"Those brown-skinned devils won't be troubling the Company again?"

"No, sir. Not in this life." Horne's voice was deep-chested but soft, surprisingly mellow for a man of his size.

"So you weren't . . . *disabled* by lack of manpower?"

"No, sir."

Watson's watery blue eyes remained fixed on Horne; he appeared to be assimilating his next question.

Finally nodding, he said, "Good. Excellent. Now I can tell you about the French."

The French? Horne did not understand. How did the French follow questions about manpower? Was Watson sending him to join the Navy blockade in the Bay of Bengal?

"Horne, the French surrendered Pondicherry."

Pondicherry was France's one remaining stronghold on the west coast of India. Horne knew, too, that the defeat of Pondicherry could mean the end of the war, at least here in India.

Watson elaborated. "General Lally surrendered two weeks ago: the sixteenth of January to be precise."

General Thomas Lally was a hot-headed Irishman who served as France's Commander-in-Chief in India, a man with a reputation for being a keen strategist. Horne had also heard quarterdeck gossip that General Lally was a drunkard, a tyrant and an insufferable snob.

Watson fanned his face with the cotton square. "I'm under strict orders, Horne," he confessed, "not to discuss Lally's surrender except to say . . ."

Horne noticed that Watson's forehead had beaded with perspiration, that his voice had lowered to a croak rather than a rasp, that he appeared to be troubled.

"Horne, the Governors of the Honourable East India Company have ordered the Bombay Marine to form a special squadron. The assignment is to be of the highest secrecy. From what I know of your record, and from what you've told me about this last mission, I know I'm right in thinking you're the man to take that squadron into Fort St. George."

Horne understood now why Watson had surprised him and was asking so many questions about land attacks: the Governors were sending Marines into the Company's best fortified post in India. But why?

"You will begin preparing a squadron immediately, Horne."

Horne thought again about lack of manpower.

"I cannot say exactly how large the squadron must be, Horne. I can only tell you that your orders are to move General Lally from Fort St. George to a merchantman sailing for England."

" 'Move'?" Horne did not understand. " 'Move' as an escort, sir?"

Watson's smile was thin, almost mocking.

"No, Horne. The action should prove to be a little more . . . lively than an escort exercise. Unfortunately, the only thing I can tell you about it at this juncture is that General Lally is being held as a prisoner-of-war in Fort St. George."

"Excuse me, sir, but I've heard that Admiral Pocock joined Colonel Coote in the siege of Pondicherry. Does that mean that the Navy holds Lally prisoner with the Army?"

Watson opened his mouth to protest at Horne's question. But pushing back his chair, he rose from the desk, saying in a burst of amazement, "Damn it, Horne. You find your way straight to the puzzle, don't you?"

Puzzle? What puzzle? Horne had asked what he considered to be an obvious question—whose prisoner was Lally? The Army's or Navy's or both?

Beginning to pace the rich oriental carpets layered on the floor of his chamber, Watson proceeded. "I repeat, Horne, that I am not allowed to divulge any information to you about Lally's surrender. You will be

given all necessary details in due course. In the mean-
time, you must act with the greatest care in preparing
your squadron."

He glanced over his shoulder at Horne. "You must
not confide in your men about the nature of this mission. Not until you have final orders to enter the fortress."

"I understand, sir."

Watson wadded the handkerchief, dabbing at his
jowls and neck. "The Lord forbid that Colonel Coote
and the Army should suspect the Company's actions.
There'll be the devil to pay, too, if Admiral Pocock
and the Admiralty get wind of this plan." He mopped
the handkerchief across his sun-blotched pate. "The devil to pay."

Commodore Watson, the Commander-in-Chief of
the Bombay Marine, was frightened of both the
Army's Colonel Coote and the Navy's Admiral Pocock. Horne was certain of it, and surprised. Commodore Watson was usually stubborn, demanding, firmly
set in his ways, a blustery old walrus. So there must
be good reasons for his sudden change of character.

Remembering Watson's calmness at the outset of the
interview, Horne recalled how the jowled old Commodore had only become nervous when he had begun
talking about Lally's imprisonment at Fort St. George.

Horne could think of only one reason for Watson's
nerves: the Governors of the East India Company had
ordered the Bombay Marine to *kidnap* Lally from his
prison at Fort St. George. And if the British Army or
Navy were holding the French Commander-in-Chief as

a prisoner-of-war, such action would, of course, be high treason.

The air in Commodore Watson's chamber remained humid and uncomfortable, despite the slight breeze raised by the *punkah* fan as it swept back and forth. Watson moved from his desk to the window, nervously mopping his brow. "You should be aware, Horne," he explained, "that your orders will continue to be verbal. You must understand, too, that if you or any of your men are apprehended during this assignment—seized and arrested either by the Army or Navy—the East India Company will not come to your defence. The Governors will deny all orders concerning Thomas Lally."

To be disowned by the Company's three Governors on a mission of their assigning neither surprised nor angered Adam Horne. His father was a London merchant banker; he had learnt from boyhood that all trading companies and their servants were by nature self-serving.

Watson's voice was regaining some of its rasping assurance, its bark. "I too will deny any knowledge of your activities at Fort St. George."

"Yes, sir."

Horne disliked officers abandoning their men. But he was relieved to hear that he was not going to be dispatched to join the Navy's blockade, that he would be operating independently of superiors—regardless of the assignment's mysterious nature.

"You're to look for no outside help at any point of

the mission, Horne. Do you thoroughly understand that point?"

"Yes, sir." Horne sat stiffly in the straight-backed chair, his cocked hat resting on his left knee.

"Any man apprehended during the mission shall be brought before a Court of Inquiry. The charge would be treason."

The mention of treason reminded Horne of his suspicions that the Company's Governors were sending the Bombay Marine to kidnap a prisoner-of-war. Could he possibly be right?

Watson stood in front of the window cut into the castle's south wall, high above the harbour, the busiest trading port in the Arabian Sea. "Horne, I learned only yesterday that a storm struck the Coromandel Coast while Lally was negotiating his surrender. I tell you this because in November I despatched the remaining three Bombay ships to Pondicherry and I've had no word of them being amongst the survivors. You probably have friends or old shipmates aboard the lost frigates and will hear of it. I also want you to know this fact because it means I cannot spare you one single man."

Instead of dwelling on the thoughts of friends lost at sea, or the chance that he might have been one of them, Horne took what seemed like the one millionth count of men aboard the *Eclipse*.

"Sir, the *Eclipse* was undermanned when I last set sail from Bombay. When you read my report, you will see that a total of twenty-two men were killed in battle. A further seven men died from yellow fever."

Watson remained by the window. Below him

brightly striped tents stretched along the stone wharf. Snub-nosed native craft and Malabar sailing boats swarmed amid the din of voices, bells and vendors' cries. Keeping his eyes on the colourful harbour confusion, he asked, "What's your present crew, Horne?"

"Eighty-nine men, sir." The number was ludicrously low even by Bombay Marine standards.

"Your Marine detachment?"

"Seventeen, sir, including Sergeant Rajit."

"These men are capable?"

"As fit as can be expected, sir. We've been fourteen months out of port."

"But not the men we need."

"No, sir. In fact, I can easily say now, sir, I have no more than three, perhaps four men whom I could recommend for any action demanding a quick mind and strong body."

Watson turned from the window, speaking as if to himself. "Damn it to hell! Why do we never have enough bloody *men*?"

Horne understood Watson's fury. He himself had grown to feel the same anger, the same unquenchable hunger, like a cat on a constant prowl for canaries.

"Sir, if I cannot recruit men in Bombay, what about Madras or Calcutta? The Company garrisons troops at both posts."

Watson shook his head. "No. Definitely not. The Governors don't want Company troops taking any part in this manoeuvre. Governor Pigot of Madras will supply us with details of Fort St. George. Governor Vansittart of Bengal will give us the information we need about the military. Governor Spencer, here in Bombay,

will turn a blind eye to any preparations we make at
the Castle. But none of the three Governors will supply
us with men. Their orders are strictly for the Marine."

"Sir, am I allowed time to train recruits if I'm lucky
enough to find them?"

"Absolutely. Men could be trained while I'm waiting
for maps and charts to be sent from Fort St. George.
The problem is to find them. The Navy had press-
ganged every man and boy from here to Calcutta."

Horne made a quick mental note of Watson's ref-
erence to waiting for maps and charts to be sent from
Fort St. George. That meant the mission would obviously be one of infiltration, a covert entry into the fortress for which they would need precise details.

"The Navy's combed all the islands for men, sir?"
he asked.

"Completely. The one place they haven't ransacked
is Mauritius, and only because the French still have
their base there."

Horne's mind went back to the *Eclipse*, scanning the
faces of his crew, wondering if by any stretch of the
imagination he could transform a few more seamen
into Marines as he had managed to do on the Maratha
campaign, and if the ship's manning would allow it.
He pictured Merlin, the gunner, barrel-chested, strong,
loyal—and irreplaceable from the gun deck. Gibbons,
the boatswain, foulmouthed and domineering—and
also necessary in casting off, weighing anchor and
countless other duties he had come to perform on the
main deck. Then there was Kevin O'Flaherty, a young
Irish leadsman who had been press-ganged from
Mount Keene Prison in Dublin . . .

An idea struck him and, weighing it for a few seconds, he decided there would be no harm in mentioning it to Watson.

"Sir, there's a prison here at Bombay Castle."

Watson glanced over his shoulder at Horne, his porcine eyes sharp with caution under his bushy eyebrows.

"Sir, there must be near two hundred men in the dungeons here."

Watson's tone was clipped. "Horne, I know what you're going to suggest but put it out of your mind. The dregs of Europe and the Orient are condemned to Bombay Castle."

Horne moved to the edge of his chair, increasingly excited by the idea. "But, sir, there must be a handful of men we can use, convicts I can train as I'd train civilian recruits."

"No, Horne. Definitely not. Men are already taken from prisons in England for too many ships during war time. That means that most of the prisoners at Bombay Castle are serving a second, some even a third or fourth prison term. What makes you think they'd obey orders from you?"

Horne was tenacious, a man who did not change his mind easily once he was convinced.

"We could offer them freedom, sir. Give them freedom and a full pardon in return for their services. Many of them probably never expect to see the light of day again, Sir. I'll train them on a disciplinary probation."

"Horne, murderers and thieves from every corner of the world are locked in the dungeons of Bombay Castle. British. Dutch. French. African. Chinese. Men who have committed crimes against the Crown as well as the Company."

Horne forgot that he was arguing with his commanding officer. He spoke to prove his point.

"Sir, I know many of the prisoners are foreign. But so are the Lascar sailors we recruit here and train for our fleets. The Navy does too."

Horne sat sideways in his chair now, his hazel eyes alert with excitement. "And consider this fact, sir. I could train the prisoners during the time you're waiting for the information from Governor Pigot."

From the window Watson watched two turbanned *dhoolie* bearers edging along the wharf as beggars, vendors, and naked children swarmed around the covered litter. "Horne, why haven't the Army and Navy raided the prisons of Bombay Castle if such a thing's possible? Answer me that."

"Perhaps, sir, for the simple reason that the thought has never occurred to them."

Horne was excited by the sudden turn in his prospects. Less than an hour ago he had been pacing the outside hallway, worrying about his future. Now here he was in Watson's office arguing about taking convicts aboard his ship.

The cocked hat still resting on his knee, he continued, "Excuse me for saying so, sir, but if we *wait* for the Navy to think of raiding our prison, there'll be no men left for us."

Watson began shaking his bald head. "Prisoners for Marines, Horne? No, it's not possible. Not possible at all. First, what proof do you have they wouldn't mutiny as soon as you're to sea?"

"Sir, does a captain ever have assurance against mutiny?"

Watson did not hear him. "And rivalries brought from prison, Horne. What about that? Convicted men are vicious, vengeful creatures."

"Are prison rivalries different, sir, from free men arguing about religion? Politics? Blood feuds?"

Adam Horne continued to meet each criticism Watson made, arguing how he might deal with desertion, subterfuge, mutiny, even contagious diseases brought from dank, pestilent cells.

Finally Watson turned from the window. "Horne," he said resignedly, "I've learnt over the years that the best way to convince a man that he's mistaken is to allow him to discover the fact for himself. That is not always possible. But in this case, it is. You can go down to the dungeons and see the men you propose to turn into Marines. Then you can come back here and say you've got the idea out of your head."

Horne detected sarcasm in Watson's voice but he didn't care.

"Thank you, sir."

"Lieutenant Todwell can supply you with a prison list as well as an armed guard."

Horne rose to his feet, the cocked hat in one hand.

"One further matter, Horne."

"Sir?"

Watson fixed his small blue eyes on Horne. "The Governors want Lally aboard that ship bound for England in six weeks' time. This mission is urgent to the Company. It could also be very important to you, Horne. The kind of assignment an independent, strong-

minded young officer like you dreams of. Something
to get your damned teeth into. But it also could be the
end of your career. So don't make it more difficult than
it already is. Do you understand what I'm saying,
Horne?"

"Yes, sir."

Watson studied Horne a few moments longer as if
he were trying to break the protective wall with which
Horne always seemed to surround himself, then he
shook his head. "Oh, the hell you understand," he ex-
claimed, waving his hand. "You're just thinking about
finding an able-bodied man or two down in that cess-
pit. So go on. Get out of here."

Horne held his salute until Watson dismissed him
officially.

After Adam Horne had left for the dungeon Commodore Watson went and stood by the window. Ignoring
the swarm of wharfside activity and the ships tangled
with fishing boats in the harbour, he stared blankly at
the hazy line of mountains far away on the Indian
mainland.

When would the three Governors allow him to tell
Horne the reason why General Lally had to be moved
from Fort St. George? But apart from being unable to
disclose full details of the mission, he was also troubled by having no men to assign to Horne for a squadron. The disappearance of one vessel gave him
nightmares; news that half his command might be
destroyed shattered him.

Watson turned from the window. He wished he had
not promised his wife, Emma, that he would stop

drinking. A gin and lemon juice would settle his nerves. But no amount of gin was worth the risk of losing the woman who had stood by him for the last forty-two years.

Watson had come out to India after retiring from a career in His Britannic Majesty's Royal Navy. Rising to Rear Admiral of the Blue in the West Indies, Watson had accepted the post of Commodore and Commander-in-Chief of the Bombay Marine rather than settle down to a dull life of raising dogs in Surrey.

But why had a young man like Adam Horne joined the Bombay Marine? Horne was young, personable, far more gifted than most officers Watson had met throughout the years. So why did not a bright young man, starting out in life, pursue a career in the Navy or the East India Company's prestigious Maritime Fleet? Why choose the rough-and-tumble, shabby Bombay Marine?

Watson knew little about Horne's private life. Company records supplied the facts that he had joined the Marine seven years ago, had risen from the rank of Midshipman to First Lieutenant aboard the *Protector*, forty-four guns, the flagship of Watson's predecessor, Commodore James, and that James had promoted Horne to Captain on his retirement.

Watson had heard gossip that Adam Horne had been involved in the murder of a young woman in a London bordello. There were stories, too, that Horne had studied as a young man with Elihu Cornhill, the eccentric old soldier who taught boys controversial ideas about survival in the wilderness.

Watson had a rule whereby he did not believe rumors about his officers. He tried to judge a man by his actions, and Adam Horne's report about the Maratha pirates fortified his opinion that Horne was a versatile leader, both on land and sea, a commander who acted responsibly for other men's lives yet was unafraid of death himself.

Over his past forty-two years of Naval service, Watson had known no more than a handful of men who were undaunted by the prospect of being killed in battle. Each and every one of those men had had a close encounter with death. The experience had left them with an advantage over fear. He suspected Adam Horne was such a man.

2

A Quick Mind
and Strong Body

Accompanied by Lieutenant Todwell and a party of
eight armed guards, Adam Horne descended deep into
the maze of dark passageways channelled into the bed-
rock beneath Bombay Castle. The clank of cutlasses
and muskets echoed with the thud of footfalls; the
moving torches sputtered in cross-currents of air, the
light illuminating bats hanging upside down from
mouldy corners, singeing spiders' webs festooned
across the low, seeping ceilings.

Lieutenant Todwell held a parchment high in front
of his eyes, catching the glow of the torch behind him
as he read, "William Bradford, *Calumet*. Judged guilty
of murdering an officer. Death by hanging . . . Henry
Denning, *City of Manchester*. Judged guilty of murdering a fellow servant. Death by hanging . . . Brian
McGregory, *Fifth Regiment of the Foot*. Judged guilty
of mutiny and pilfering medical supplies. Thirty-five
years imprisonment . . ."

Moving down a chilly incline, Adam Horne stopped listening to Todwell reading the prison list and began reappraising the scant information Commodore Watson had given him about the mission to Fort St. George.

Had the East India Company's Governors of India's three Presidencies—Bengal, Bombay, and Madras—ordered the mission for the reason Horne suspected? To abduct an important prisoner-of-war from the Army or Navy? If so, what was their motive? To claim valuable war prizes for the Company?

The East India Company was rich, vastly rich. Their merchant ships profited well over three hundred per cent from voyages to the Orient, bringing home silks, spices, teas; indigo for dyes, saltpetre for gunpowder, baubles for the British housewives.

Chartered by Queen Elizabeth more than a hundred-and-seventy years ago, in 1600, the East India Company had surpassed the Dutch and Portuguese traders in world markets. Investors streamed to the Company's headquarters on Leadenhall Street in London to buy shares in every new voyage.

No, Horne decided, the East India Company would not be abducting France's Commander-in-Chief to claim war prizes. The Company had more wealth—and power—than most nations. And France's own East India Company—the *Compagnie des Indes Orientales*—had declined in the last few years, changing the war between England and France from a struggle for trade monopoly to a battle for territory.

So, if the Governors' reason for sending a squadron of Marines to kidnap Lally was not financial, why would they be ordering a secret mission? For military reasons?

Military strength was becoming an increasing concern of the East India Company. It was learning quickly that its profits were larger with the help of the sword and cannon. And not all of the Company's present battles were being waged against the French.

The present Governor of Bengal was Henry Vansittart. His predecessor, Robert Clive, had led the British Army against Indian troops, defeating the Nawab of Bengal four years ago at Plassey, securing Bengal as a monopoly for East India Company traders. The Army had bestowed the title of Major on Robert Clive for his victory, the first time an employee of the East India Company had also held a commission in the Royal Army.

Walking deeper into the underground maze beneath Bombay Castle, Adam Horne wondered if the Company's three Governors might be trying to follow Robert Clive's example. Clive had returned to London where he was being hailed as a military hero as well as the richest man in the world from his Indian war prizes. The present Governors might have similar ambitions, using Horne's squadron to lay the groundwork.

The air grew more chilly the deeper the armed party moved underground. Horne braced himself against the change of temperature, realizing that he was foolish to waste time speculating about the motives of his superiors.

He had two choices of action. Either to obey orders, or to break the Oath of Allegiance he had sworn to serve King and Company.

• • •

He halted the small band of armed guards on the third
subterranean level beneath Bombay Castle, stopping in
front of an iron grille flanked by two smoking torches
held by iron wall brackets.

Behind the grille, a squat turnkey saluted. "Sergeant
Suggins, sir."

Horne touched his hat and stepped aside for Lieutenant Todwell to hand the written pass through the
bars.

Sergeant Suggins took the pass and moved his
greasy lips as he read the Commodore's orders. Pushing back the paper through the bars, he lifted a large
ring of iron keys from his belt, unlocked the grille and
stood aside for the party to file past him. Relocking
the gate, he hurried to join them as they continued
down to the fourth level.

Horne slowed to speak to Suggins. "Tell me, Sergeant, how does the count of one-hundred-and-eleven
men compare with your tally of prisoners?"

Suggins puffed to keep pace with Horne. "With all
due respects, sir, I'm the turnkey and not required to
keep roll muster."

Horne frowned. He disliked people who refused to
give help beyond the bounds of duty. Was it a trait
common only amongst the English? Or did this annoying, lazy breed of man exist in all nations of the world?

"Sergeant Suggins, I imagine some prisoners are less
troublesome, quieter than others. I'd like you to point
out those men to me."

"Ah, now, sir, a quiet man's the man to watch out
for, isn't he? That's the fellow you find hanging by his

shirt tail. A quiet man's always the man who does himself in."

Horne considered himself to be a quiet man, an introspective man, some people even called him moody. But he certainly did not consider himself to be a man who'd take his own life. He fought too hard—too often—to stay alive.

Forcing himself to be patient with the turnkey's annoying observations, he pressed, "You must have noticed ringleaders amongst the prisoners, Sergeant Suggins. Men who rise above others. Distinguish themselves in some way."

"Aye, sir. You're talking about the bullies."

"Sergeant, it's the bullies I want you to point out to me first."

"May I ask, sir, the reason for this visit?"

Horne knew he might need the turnkey's cooperation in the next few days. He suspected that Suggins was the kind of man to undermine a superior officer's work if he was too severely rebuked.

Forcing himself to be diplomatic, he answered, "A man of your position, Sergeant, certainly respects confidential orders."

"Yes, sir. Of course, sir."

The armed party halted in front of a second grille, the torches catching shapes of men crowding inside the bars, the flickering light showing unkempt hair, ragged beards, filthy clothing, grimy hands gripping the iron bars.

Sergeant Suggins snatched the leather cudgel from his belt and began jabbing its spiked head back and forth between the bars. "Back, you scum, or there'll be no supper for any of you tonight."

A lanky prisoner pressed his face between the bars. "No supper, guv'nor? You mean to rob us of all our tasty morsels?"

Another prisoner shoved his head close to Suggins, the lower half of his round face bushy with red whiskers. "Don't rob us of our supper, Sergeant. We're just getting a taste for that rat dung!"

More taunts, more coarse laughter surrounded Suggins as he unlocked the grille. Ignoring the prisoners, he motioned the guards forward with their bayonets.

Horne followed the guards through the open grille, estimating that there must be two dozen, perhaps as many as thirty prisoners locked in this first cell, at least a third of the men having oriental features.

Looking towards the next grille, he saw a body sprawled on the floor a few yards in front of him. A dark fluid covered the prisoner's chest, thick and reddish in the torchlight.

Suggins spied the body and moved to kick him. "Up, lazy pig."

Horne reached quickly to stop him. "The man's bleeding, Sergeant."

"Aye, sir. Bleeding from a fight." Suggins surveyed the other prisoners gathering across the cell from him. His eyes rested on a tall man with big ears standing apart from the group and he pointed his cudgel at him. "There's the dog he was fighting with, Captain. Look at those hands."

Horne saw the glimmer of blood on the other prisoner's hands. He raised his eyes above the man's chest to see a thin, challenging smirk. Suggins was probably right. Looking back to the blood-covered man on the floor, he beckoned a torch-bearer and dropped to his knees.

Suggins moved behind him. "Sir, show no mercy for these dogs."

Horne's patience was wearing thin. "Sergeant, keep the prisoners against the far wall."

Turning back to the injured man, he reached to feel his pulse. At the same moment, the blood-covered prisoner sprang upward with a knife.

Clutching Horne by the uniform, the prisoner jabbed the rusty blade at his throat. "Tell the Sergeant to throw me his keys, Captain, or I'll slice you earhole to earhole."

Horne cursed his stupidity.

"Those keys!" The prisoner pressed the knife against Horne's throat. "Tell your fat Sergeant to toss me those keys."

Behind Horne, Suggins whined, "I said not to help him, Captain."

"Sergeant Suggins, do as this man says. Toss him your keys."

Sergeant Suggins stood a few yards behind Adam Horne in the cell, looking from the blood-covered prisoner holding the knife to Horne's throat to the ragged prisoners crowded in front of the guards' bayonets. His reply was a nervous belch.

Horne demanded louder. "Suggins, the keys. Throw the man your keys."

"I warned you, Captain, not to help—"

"Suggins, the keys."

Grudgingly, Suggins lifted the iron ring of keys from his belt and tossed them across the cell.

Keeping the blade at Horne's neck, the prisoner reached to catch the keys.

Horne moved faster.

Grabbing the keys, he slapped at the prisoner's knife, sending it clattering across the floor. Then, straddling the surprised man, he pressed the long keys down onto his face, raking the iron prongs across his eyes and leaving a scarlet track like the claw marks of a large cat. As he sprang to his feet, he snatched the knife from the floor.

The prisoner lay holding his face. "I can't see! You blinded me! I can't see! *I can't see*!"

Horne ignored the cries, studying the knife, a rusty blade secured to a large bone by a wiry substance. What was it? Thin wire? Coarse thread? Hair?

Tucking the knife into his waistband, he ordered, "Lieutenant Todwell, line these men against the wall."

Todwell beckoned the guards forward.

Horne stepped towards the prisoner with big ears and blood smeared on his hands.

"I presume you were part of this game."

The prisoner nodded, returning Horne's glare.

"What's your name?"

The prisoner remained silent, his jaw firmly set.

Horne snatched the crudely made knife from his waistband. "Name, damn you!"

The man's confidence weakened. "Babcock . . ."

Horne's temper was frayed. "Don't you know how to address an officer, Babcock?"

"Yes . . ."

"Yes, *who*?"

"Yes . . . sir."

"Where are you from, Babcock?"

"The Colonies. The American Colonies. The Ohio Valley . . . sir."

"What's your crime, Babcock?"

"Striking an officer. On the *White Plover* out of Boston sailing for Madagascar. But I didn't do it. I'm not guilty . . . sir."

"Do you *want* to do it, Babcock?"

Babcock's big ears twitched, his brow wrinkling.

"Do you want to strike an officer, Babcock? If so, now's your chance to do it. You better take it because you're not going to get it again."

Babcock glanced at the other prisoners.

"Come on, Babcock. You want to do it. So come on. Hit me."

"No . . . sir."

"Don't be a coward, Babcock."

"I'm not a coward . . ." Babcock faltered, shaking his head.

Horne corrected, " 'I'm not a coward, *sir*!' Say it, Babcock." He held Babcock's eyes, defying him to strike, taunting, "Say it, Babcock. Or else show me you aren't afraid to hit me."

"Don't push me . . . *sir*."

Horne smiled. "Good, Babcock." He raised the knife. "Now tell me how this got in here, Babcock."

Babcock nodded to the man lying on the floor holding his eyes. "That was Gilbert's idea. Gilbert sneaked the blade into the cell inside his beard. Then he cut off his beard and used the whiskers to tie the blade to an old bone for a handle."

Horne nodded his approval; details fascinated him; ingenuity was a man's fuel for survival.

Tucking the crudely-made weapon back into his waistband, he asked, "What about the blood on your hands, Babcock? How did that get there?"

"A bloody nose. It's easy to make a nose bleed, isn't it?"

"But more than one nose."

The big American Colonial nodded.

"So you had a small conspiracy here, Babcock."

"That could be one name for it . . . sir."

"How did you know we were coming?"

"These caverns echo. We heard you a mile or two away."

"Whose idea was the ambush?"

A grin cracked Babcock's unshaven face. "I always understand it's not polite to brag . . . sir."

Keeping his eyes on the beefy, big-eared American Colonial Horne called, "Lieutenant Todwell, Mr. Babcock here appears to have two of the qualities I'm looking for in a recruit. A quick mind and strong body. Enter his name at the top of the list."

He shoved Babcock towards the wall and shouted to the other prisoners, "All right, the rest of you make a line. The tallest to the shortest. The first man who disobeys orders joins his friend behind me on the floor. Now *move!*"

Bare feet scuffed quickly over the floor.

3

The Eclipse

The morning wind swept away all trace of cloud from
the Indian sky. The gale was still rising, chopping
Bombay's harbour into silver-capped waves, making
the air fresh and Adam Horne pleased to be once again
aboard the *Eclipse*.

Climbing the ladder to the quarterdeck, Horne
watched the crew gathering below the masts. Ten days
back in Bombay had apparently raised the men's spirits.

Bombay was a congested, noisy settlement built
around the bastions of Bombay Castle. It was not un-
usual for East India Company officials and their wives
to complain about the growing city. English families
found its accommodation crude, its social life boring,
compared to the busy whirl of Calcutta and Madras.

But a seaman in search of a good time found many
lusty diversions in Bombay, from dockside cafés serving coarse liquor called "arrack," to the narrow, wind-

ing alleyways crammed with warrens of brightly painted rooms where dancing-girls entertained strangers for a few copper *pisces*.

Horne had expected the crew to complain about embarking so soon after returning from the last mission. But when he had been piped aboard the *Eclipse* shortly after dawn, he had been greeted with neat, crisp salutes from the men, all uniformly dressed in new white shirts and wide trousers sewn from blue Indian cloth called "*dungri*."

He had also noticed that his two Midshipmen, Jeremy Bruce and Calvin Mercer, seemed pleased with their new uniforms, waist jackets cut with small round sleeves and brass buttons sewn on the cuffs. Perhaps the East India Company knew how to please men better than Horne suspected they did.

First Lieutenant Pilkington stepped towards Horne on the quarterdeck. "Stores secure, sir."

Horne touched his hat, seeing that his first officer, Ronald Pilkington, looked smart in his own new uniform, a frock coat trimmed with yellow facing and gold braid.

"Pilkington, sixteen prisoners from Bombay Castle were boarded during the night. Have they been fed this morning?"

"Aye, aye, sir." Pilkington stood as tall as Adam Horne, blue-eyed, eager to please, and fastidious. "Sergeant Rajit has the new men chained on the orlop deck, sir."

Horne was impressed that Pilkington did not try to find out why prisoners were aboard the *Eclipse*. The First Lieutenant had obviously learnt at last that his

Captain was full of surprises but would not answer any questions until he was ready.

"Lieutenant, I presume Mr. Bruce and Mr. Mercer will not be sleeping on the orlop deck."

"No, sir. They've moved their hammocks to the forecastle, sir."

"Fine." Horne was pleased that his young officers were as adaptable as the crew.

He filled his lungs with fresh air. "Lieutenant. I'm ready to make way."

"Aye, aye, sir."

"We'll lay a starboard tack past Elephant Rock. With this wind, I gauge sou-west by west."

Horne turned towards Midshipman Bruce waiting abaft the mizzenmast. "Signal shore, Mr. Bruce. The *Eclipse* is prepared to proceed."

"Aye, aye, sir." Jeremy Bruce, a sandy-haired son of a Manchester shopkeeper, had proved in the last mission that he could turn his hand to many tasks and now served as Horne's flagman.

The signal flags were rolled into tight balls, quickly moving up the halyard, bursting into brightly coloured pennants in the wind.

Horne shaded his eyes against the sun as he studied the westerly turret of Bombay Castle. Hopefully, Commodore Watson was watching from the flag tower to answer with a personal reply. Watson had given Horne strong support in the last ten days, having argued with Governor Spencer for the Bombay Marine to recruit men from the Company's prison, and for Horne to have time and a suitable place to train the new men to become part of the mission to Fort St. George.

Governor Spencer of Bombay was a conservative man, a conventional, dedicated man who had come to India many years ago as a lowly writer for the East India Company. He had immediately resisted the idea of freeing convicts from Bombay Castle. But Watson had cajoled, even bullied him, using Horne's recent victory in the North Arabian Sea as the main basis of his argument. Spencer had finally agreed to the proposal, allowing Horne to take sixteen men from the prison. He had also prepared an official document authorizing the despatch of the *Eclipse* to a remote island in The Laccadive cluster of islands. Commodore Watson promised to join Horne in four weeks' time to inspect the new men and supply Horne with the final details of the mission.

As the signal flags fluttered in their hoists, Horne considered the island which Governor Spencer had chosen for their temporary base.

Officially, the Governor was sending Horne to reclaim an uninhabited dot in the Indian Ocean named in honour of a Company navigator, Alfred Bull. Knowing a few facts about the history of Bull Island, Horne feared what might be waiting for them there.

Midshipman Bruce reported, "Sir, Bombay Castle replies: *'Go in the name of God, King, and Company.'* "

Horne stood by the taffrail and weighed the reply. If he and his men were apprehended from this point onward, a Military Court of Inquiry could subpoena the record of Commodore Watson's last flag call to the *Eclipse* and find nothing but an innocuous message to a captain. Safe orders. An uninhabited island in the

Laccadives. Prisoners boarded under the protection of night. Yes, the departure was neat, tidy, and extremely cautious, protecting Watson, Spencer, the East India Company, everyone except the men whose lives would be in danger.

Lieutenant Pilkington's voice broke Horne's reflections. "Anchors hove short, sir."

Horne remembered his decision not to speculate, only to obey orders.

"Loose tops'ls, Lieutenant."

The command echoed through the shrouds of the *Eclipse*, the men's shouts quickly becoming louder in rapid repetition, and soon the top hands ran across the canvas and riggings, making the frigate's peaks come alive against the cloudless morning sky. Small figures of men swung on the yards, tugging at tackle and sail, freeing the halyards, canvas threatening to take shape from a pushing wind.

Tom Gibbons, the ginger-whiskered boatswain, shouted at the forecastle hands pulling the anchor. "Heave, you damned old women! Heave!"

The cable began to grate against the weight of the anchor. Gibbons cursed louder at the tugging men and, soon, the anchor bumped inward, dripping sea water, dragging a trail of slimy green weed.

Midshipman Bruce reported to Horne, "Anchor's weighed, sir."

Overhead, the wind puffed at the sails, canvas opening up and down the frigate's three masts—sky sails, top sails, royals, all popping with the force. And with the succession of loud snaps, the *Eclipse* took her first lurch, the deck canting, the sails thundering.

Adam Horne's stomach jumped as the ship moved forward on the wind. Looking overhead, he saw the hands racing to top gallants and courses, the sails opening like a white flower in sunlight, a chorus of calls accompanying this spectacle which he never ceased to find magnificent.

Lieutenant Pilkington returned to Horne's side. "Wind holds strong, sir."

"Lay the course to weather the headland."

"Aye, aye, sir."

Horne felt energy coursing through his body, a tonic he found only at sea; his muscles were already beginning to relax, his mind snapping clear of the demands and trying formalities of Bombay Castle. As the ocean spray cooled his face, he watched the hands in the forecastle drawing the headsail sheets, bringing around the *Eclipse*. Strangely, he felt pride that so few hands could man the frigate when necessary. Their performance was somehow an extention of himself. Despite their ability, though, he knew that one of his first duties must be to rearrange watch duties. He would begin by dispensing with the luxury of a dog watch.

Noticing that the wind was rising too quickly, lunging heavily into the sails, he glanced at George Tandimmer standing at the wheel, seeing that his Sailing Master was also keeping his eye on the canvas.

George Tandimmer was one of Horne's best men. Horne approved of the way Tandimmer did not hang the turn as he held a starboard tack, allowing the head to decrease a point and then to gain force with the rudder to hold onto the course.

Satisfied with Tandimmer's control of the *Eclipse*, Horne felt assured that he could leave him to continue getting under way as he himself retired to his cabin to attend to more pressing duties.

"Lieutenant Pilkington, I want to see you and Sergeant Rajit in my cabin."

He turned to descend the ladder from the quarter-deck, noticing that the wind was still rising.

Adam Horne's cabin was like no other place on the face of the earth to him. The pitch of the deck; the creak of timber as the ship tilted and dipped to the toss of the sea; the oddments of cabin fixtures, from the thin mattress slung across leather straps in the berth to the wide mahogany desk splintered in one corner by a cannonball fired from a Tamil raider's twelve pounder. Cluttered and dishevelled and smelling of tar and salt water, Horne's cabin was also the closest thing to a home he had known in the last three years—perhaps in all his seven years in India.

Lieutenant Pilkington stood alongside Marine Sergeant Rajit facing Horne's desk. Horne sat with his back to the mullioned stern windows as he explained the few bits of information he was allowed by Commodore Watson and Governor Spencer to divulge to his officers about the posting to Bull Island.

"We're sailing down the Malabar Coast, then southwest for a small island in the group of islands called The Laccadives. I'll make an official announcement later this morning."

Horne saw no flicker of curiosity in either Pilkington's or Rajit's eyes. Good men, he thought.

"Bull Island has been abandoned for more than ten years," he continued. "The Company's considering it as a training ground. We're to make repairs on its few existing buildings."

How plausible did this story sound to Pilkington and Rajit? There was a war raging with France and half of the Marine fleet had been lost in a storm off the coast of Pondicherry. Under such circumstances, would Commodore Watson despatch a thirty-six gun frigate to make *repairs* on the tumbledown buildings of an abandoned island in the middle of the Arabian Sea? Did this deceit insult his men's intelligence?

Horne proceeded with the excuse he had been given.

"As you men know, we returned from the Gulf to headquarters badly under strength. I received Commodore Watson's permission to induct sixteen men from the prisons of Bombay Castle. We're to train those men in the next few weeks. If they do not prove fit to join our Marine unit, they'll become part of the crew."

Horne looked at Sergeant Rajit. "In four weeks' time, Commodore Watson will arrive on Bull Island to inspect the new men. That does not leave us much time to get them into shape."

Sergeant Rajit, an Indian soldier trained by Europeans, a Sepoy, was a short, strongly built, man from the Punjab. Rajit excelled in drilling recruits. He could also read and write, and his diction was more precise than that of most of the British seamen aboard the *Eclipse*.

Horne studied Rajit's pudgy brown face. "Do you understand the orders, Sergeant?"

"Yes, suh!"

Horne looked back at Pilkington. "Lieutenant, I want every able-bodied man aboard the *Eclipse* to participate in the training of these new men."

"Yes, sir."

Horne hesitated before explaining the presence of another new man aboard the *Eclipse*, an old Irishman whom Watson had foisted off onto him yesterday, one day before departure.

"Commodore Watson assigned us a ship's surgeon. His name's Tim Flannery. I've given him the ward-room cabin. Lieutenant, I want you to find an assistant for Mr Flannery."

"Yes, sir."

Horne rose from behind the desk. "Assemble the crew now, Lieutenant."

Pilkington raised his salute.

Horne looked at the Sepoy Sergeant of the frigate's Marine Battalion. "Sergeant Rajit, bring the prisoners to deck."

"Suh!"

"I shall join you shortly, gentlemen."

Horne returned their salute.

"It's a pleasure to be sailing with you again, Sergeant Rajit."

"Thank you, Lieutenant Pilkington. I likewise look forward to the privilege of your company on this voyage."

"I might be imposing on your store of reading matter again, Sergeant. After enjoying your copy of Delmore's *World of Vasco Da Gama* I am eager to see what other distinguished works you have in your locker."

"Feel at liberty to ask, sir. I have a new volume which might interest you even more than the Delmore book. It's Cartwright's *History of Oriental Music*."

Lieutenant Pilkington and Sergeant Rajit emerged from the companionway, both men stiffly formal with one another despite the fact that they had spent fourteen months aboard the same ship in the North Arabian Sea.

Pilkington was still surprised to find that a native, albeit a Sepoy Sergeant, could not only read English so well but travelled with such an impressive library of expensively bound books.

Sergeant Rajit was astounded to learn that Pilkington appreciated Indian music, that he did not complain that the *ragas* played upon a sitar had no Western harmonies, that he actually seemed to understand the meaning of *rasa*, the mood of a *raga*, the flavour which most Europeans found incomprehensible. "Perhaps, Sergeant, you can interest Captain Horne in one of your books."

Pilkington's remark surprised Rajit, but the Lieutenant held his head aloft, trying to sound casual. "Captain Horne takes life so seriously. Does not allow himself to enjoy life's little pleasures. I believe that reading would put a smile on his face. Musical and literary discussion might take some of the weight of the world off Captain Horne's shoulders."

Pilkington loved to talk. About anything. Rajit knew that. He also knew that Horne seldom allowed Pilkington to talk on the quarterdeck.

Stopping at the end of the companionway, Rajit faced Pilkington and snapped a salute. "Suh!" He did not want to become involved in discussion with—or about—his superior officers.

Alone in the cabin, Horne sank back into his chair, black boots crossed in front of him beneath the desk, staring at the waterproof leather envelopes heaped in front of him. They contained official commands for Bull Island, reports of stores loaded aboard the *Eclipse*, dockyard reports of repairs completed on the frigate.

Looking from the desk to the brass-bound sea chests dotted around the cabin, Horne realized how badly he needed someone to unpack for him, a steward to bring him meals at the desk, keep his clothes washed and in relatively good repair, to perform small chores while he himself tended to more demanding tasks.

Horne's last steward had been killed by a broadside in the Gulf of Makran. There had been three other men killed the same afternoon but Horne missed Geoff Wheeler the most. He knew his reasons were purely selfish but he missed him nonetheless.

A knock on the door disturbed Horne's reverie. He grabbed his hat, ready to inspect the new men.

Stopping in front of the small bullseye mirror fastened inside the cabin door, he squared the hat on his head and fleetingly thought about who might miss him if a broadside claimed his life. Was it only commanding officers—and loved ones—who mourned men killed at sea? If so, who would grieve for him?

He turned from the mirror, wondering if this morbid thought was another facet of the desolation which had begun troubling him on the last voyage. He hoped not. He had wanted to leave all thoughts of death and mourning behind him in London when he had buried Isabel Springer. The senseless death of his fiancée still pained him, creating a dark chasm in his soul. He felt that the energy he used to fight his grief sapped any cheer he could be showing to the world, making him appear cold and uncaring, brittle to his fellow men.

Nothing chilled a man more than witnessing death; reaching for the cabin's door handle, Horne thought of more recent deaths he had seen close at hand, strangers whom he and his men had killed on Company orders, enemies of the Honourable East India Company.

Did killing under order remove the ignominy of taking a human life? Raise it above murder?

This mission to Bull Island and Madras was young, but Horne had already blinded one man at Bombay Castle. The action had been savage, true, but it had also quickly established his authority. The impulse to act in such a manner had come quickly to him, rising from his impulsive nature. Did this mean he was more savage than he had ever considered himself to be?

Remembering how he had decided not to speculate about orders given to him by superior officers, he stepped out into the companionway, telling himself that neither must he question his instinct to kill, blind, or maim. Those instincts might prove to be the difference between the success or failure of a mission, or the saving of his own life. If savagery troubled him, he must remember that his father kept a banking job for him in the landlocked safety of Lombard Street, London.

4

Roll Muster

The sun remained hot in the morning sky but the Arabian Sea was quickly turning grey and murky. The wind was growing stronger, making the *Eclipse* rise on the swells, tilt to starboard, hold for a count, then creak back to vertical before mounting the next swell.

The ragged prisoners stumbled seasick from the hatch, squinting their eyes in the sun's brightness before running across the canting deck to double over the scuppers and vomit their breakfast.

The crew gathered on gangways between the forecastle and quarterdeck, laughing at the misery of the sixteen new men who had not developed their sea legs. Lieutenant Pilkington demanded order as Sergeant Rajit sent his Marines to assemble the prisoners for roll muster.

Adam Horne, emerging from the companionway, noticed the tossing whitecaps beyond the ship's bow and guessed that a gale was strengthening off the Bombay Low. Deciding it was too soon to worry, he turned his attention back to the prisoners, the first time he had seen them in the harsh light of day.

Roll muster began with Martin Allen, a wiry man in his late twenties with a mop of yellow hair. Horne watched Allen touch his forehead as Pilkington called his name and step neatly back into line. He remembered that Allen had been a petty officer aboard a Company merchant ship. The young seaman was also a bare-knuckle fighter and had been imprisoned for killing his opponent in a match on the outward voyage from Gravesend.

Fred Babcock answered with a shout. The big-eared American Colonial did not appear to be as self-assured as when Horne had first seen him in the prison. But Babcock still looked fit and healthy, brawny and towering, hopefully good material for a Bombay Marine.

Bapu was taller, more broad-chested than most Asians Horne had met. He wore a red rag tied around his greasy black shanks of hair, and his small, dark, piercing black eyes were spaced closely together on his tawny face. Coming from Rajasthan, Bapu had led a band of thieves against Company supply caravans travelling between Jodhpur and Delhi, and he spoke fluent English. Horne had required that each man he recruited from prison should speak at least a little English.

Eid was a ship-builder from Oman. Thin and swarthy, he looked better in daylight than he had in the torchlit prison beneath Bombay Castle. Skilful with wood, canvas, and coir, the swarthy Omani was also a knifeman, quick, coolheaded, and deadly. Horne watched Eid standing in line and saw him exchanging glances with the man next to him. Were they friends? Horne had been cautious not to choose too many prisoners from the same cell. Or had a camaraderie only developed between these two men since they had been boarded last night?

Kiro was a compactly-built Japanese gunner, a captive from a pirate boat out of Nagasaki. Horne had read in Kiro's prison report that he had learnt to speak English from a Lascar sailor. It also disclosed that he had killed a fellow prisoner at Bombay Castle with one lethal chop of the hand. Horne knew of the Japanese martial art of *Karate*, understanding it to be similar to the Ancient Greek combat form, *Pankration*, which he himself had learnt as a young pupil of the retired soldier, Elihu Cornhill. Would he and Kiro ever contest their strength, *Karate* against *Pankration*, Japanese against Greek?

Dirk Groot was the one prisoner who did not appear to Horne to be seasick. But Groot's pale, Dutch complexion had blanched to a sickly pallor after being confined to the sunless dungeon of Bombay Castle. Having been gaoled for robbing a wagon of Saidabad silk which he had negotiated to sell through Dutch traders Groot had already served two-and-a-half years of a twenty-year sentence.

The smallest of Horne's sixteen prisoners was Jingee, a neat, trim, courtly Tamil from the east coast of India. Jingee had been a dubash—secretary and translator—to the English factor in Hyderabad. The Company official had chained an Indian of the high *Brahmin* caste to a lowly *Panchama* worker and ordered them to pull a plough together in his kitchen garden. When the Englishman stubbornly refused to listen to Jingee's pleas that a *Brahmin* was a priest, a figure of great respect in India, Jingee plunged a knife into the foreigner's heart.

Ted Malloy, a British sailor with a short pigtail, had been recruited into His Majesty's Royal Navy from the Crown Prison in Bristol. Horne had chosen Ted Malloy because of the knowledge of explosives he had acquired in the Navy. He had chosen only one other man who had been previously imprisoned, the British man with burning black eyes who next stepped forward to identify himself—Kevin McFiddich.

The stocky Turk with a thick black moustache, Mustafa, identified himself by raising his arm and simultaneously dropping his head as if he were ashamed. Why? Did Mustafa feel humiliated at being a prisoner? Or was the Turk embarrassed that he had vomited, considering seasickness a slur against his masculinity? Whatever the reason, Horne knew from Mustafa's prison record that he was masterly with a garrotte.

Jud Mwambi's ebony skin glistened in the bright sunlight as he stepped forward, exposing a wide expanse of pearly white teeth. This African giant could scale the highest wall if there was something he wanted badly enough. Horne had tested Jud's climbing ability in prison, and he planned to make good use of this thief both at sea and on land.

Gerard Poiret, skilled with a strongbow, threw out his bare chest and identified himself with military crispness. He was a Frenchman who had killed an English Second Lieutenant who had stolen his wife.

The roll call proceeded. Horne closely scrutinized

the men answering to the names of Jim Pugh, Edward Quinte, Brian Scott, and Fernando Vega. Looking at each one, he searched for some clue to who might become a Marine or a sailor, and who might be the man to spark trouble.

As Lieutenant Pilkington completed roll muster, Horne stepped forward. Standing with his boots wide apart, hands gripped behind his back, he studied the sixteen shabby men lined in front of him, an oddly matched collection of scowling faces, squinting eyes, ragged beards.

"Any man trying to escape will be killed on the spot."

The announcement was dramatic but Horne was pleased to see he instantly had everybody's full attention.

"If any man manages to escape, the rest of you will be sent back to prison. So it's to your advantage to stop all escape attempts."

The prisoners glanced at one another.

"We're sailing for Bull Island."

The *Eclipse* lifted on a swell, tipped, and creaked back again on the creaming dark sea.

"Bull Island used to belong to the French. It was settled by a man named Dupleix. Does anyone know who he was?"

Horne scanned the dirty, unshaven faces. Not even the French prisoner, Poiret, showed a flicker of recognition at the mention of the name.

"Dupleix was France's first Commander out here. He coined the phrase *Le Grande Jeu* for India. He also applied it to the island where we're sailing. For those men who don't understand French, *Le Grande Jeu* means 'The Great Game.' Dupleix obviously had a rather twisted sense of humour. The island was a French penal colony. Its prison and torture racks were far from being a 'great game.' At least for the prisoners."

Murmurs now passed through the crew.

Horne kept his eyes on his new recruits. "Why am I taking you from one prison to another? The answer's simple. I want your muscle. Your skills. We have to rebuild Bull Island."

He nodded towards the gangways. "The other men will tell you we put our backs to every task aboard this ship. They'll tell you, too, that I don't believe in punishment. Not severe punishment. I believe there's a better way to get work and obedience from a man than flogging him to death. But any man who disobeys me will suffer the consequences. And I'll tell you all now that those consequences are numerous and definitely no 'game.' "

The prisoners glanced at the crew.

Horne raised his voice, speaking loud and clear, not at all uncomfortable that some of the men he was threatening might be stronger than himself, or a few old enough to be his father.

"You will learn that I don't hold store with rank and ceremony. I don't pretend this is a ship of His Majesty's Navy. By the same token, I expect my orders to be obeyed and all my officers to be shown absolute respect.

"Life on Bull Island won't be easy for any of us.

Everybody will get more than his fair share of work. Hard work. Eighteen hours a day of work.

"Those new men who survive Bull Island will be granted a full pardon for their crime. They will be sworn in as Bombay Marines, to serve as members of the ship's crew or as—" Horne nodded at Sergeant Rajit's line of soldiers standing ramrod stiff, the butts of their muskets resting on the deck in front of their boots "—or as members of the ship's Marine battalion."

He looked back at the prisoners.

"I have left Writs of Freedom with all your names on them at Bombay Castle. Upon my recommendation those Writs will be counter-signed by Governor Spencer and you will be free men.

"Likewise, I can request that those documents be destroyed and any or every one of you sent back to the prison.

"Also, it may interest you new men to know that if *I* don't return from this mission, those Writs of Freedom will be destroyed and you will be returned to prison. So it does not take a wise man to figure out that it's to all your advantage that I stay alive."

Horne raised his eyes aloft, looking at the topgallant billowed in the growing wind. "Now, if any man has a question, this is the time to ask it."

As the sea slapped against the hull, sending fine sheets of spray above the bulwark, Horne looked at the line of prisoners, at Rajit's file of Marines, at the crew gathered on the gangways.

"Anybody have a question?"

Tom Gibbons, the barrel-chested boatswain, called

from the forecastle, "Sir, do we stay at this Bull Island too?"

"Are you part of my company, Gibbons?"

"Aye, aye, sir, and proud to say so."

"Then you stay at Bull Island."

"Aye, aye, sir."

Merlin the gunner rose from a capstan. "Sir, you mention that there's work to be done on Bull Island. What kind of work, sir?"

"Repairing buildings. Mending roofs. Rebuilding fortifications. We'll know more when we get there, Merlin."

"What do we get, sir, for doing this extra work, sir? Us of the ship's crew?"

"Forty lashes if you *don't* work, Merlin."

Laughter greeted Horne's quick response.

Horne turned his head to Sergeant Rajit. "Sergeant, inform your men that a Marine also does his duty and expects no bonus or reward."

Rajit saluted.

Horne clarified. "Both at sea *and* on land, Sergeant."

"Suh!"

Horne glanced at the prison column. "Any questions here?"

The tow-headed Dutchman stepped forward, neatly saluting, identifying himself, "Dirk Groot, *schupper*."

The title *schupper* was Dutch for Captain. Horne knew it was creeping into the English language as "skipper" and he allowed Groot the freedom to use it in addressing him.

Horne returned the salute. "What's your question, Groot?"

"*Schupper*, you say 'Marine,' but what kind of Marine do you mean? Is this the English King's Marine?"

For the first time smiles cracked below the tall shakos of Rajit's Marines as laughter spread through the rest of the ship.

Permitting the men their fun, Horne finally raised his voice to silence them. "Groot, Holland was the first country to send an organized trading company to the East Indies. England and the rest of the world followed. The English East India Company is controlled by a group of rich tradesmen and not the Crown. So the English Company has a private Marine to protect their trading ships instead of the King's forces. That's who we are, Groot. The trading company's troops. The Bombay Marine. A private navy of sailors and military financed by the East India Company to protect their merchant ships."

"Sir, are the men of the Bombay Marine like . . . like . . ." Groot raised his head as if thinking of the correct English word or phrase, ". . . like . . . soldiers of fortune?"

"Soldiers of fortune, Groot, usually fight for a country. We are employed by a company. Our leader is a Commodore. Our headquarters is at Bombay Castle. That's where we get our name. The Bombay Marine. But the men of the force are called Marines. The Bombay Marines."

A voice shouted from the opposite end of the prisoner column. "The Bombay Buccan*eeeeers*!"

Horne looked and saw the big-eared American Colonial grinning in the prison line.

"That's right, Babcock. Other forces have a low

opinion of the Company's Marine and call us 'Buc-caneers.' And to thank you for sharing your knowledge with us this morning, Babcock, I'm going to grant you a very special privilege."

The grin widened on Babcock's unshaven face.

"Do you know what a ship's Bible is, Babcock?"

"A Bible?"

"A ship's Bible, Babcock."

Babcock shook his head.

"Have you lost your voice, Babcock?"

"No."

"Have you forgotten again how to address an officer, Babcock?"

"No . . . sir."

"Very good, Babcock. Now where was I?"

"You were giving me a special privilege . . . sir."

"Ah, yes, Babcock. The ship's Bible."

Horne began nodding his head, moving across the tilting deck towards Babcock. "A ship's Bible, Bab-cock, is something a man holds whilst kneeling on deck. You've been to sea before so you might know it under it's other name: a holystone. Something you scrub the deck with. And every morning, Babcock, you're going to get down on your knees and holystone the deck. Do you understand, Babcock."

Babcock's face flushed a deep red.

Horne asked louder. "Do you understand, Babcock?"

"Yes, sir. Aye, aye, sir."

"Good, Babcock."

Horne turned to Pilkington. "I leave these men to you now, Lieutenant. Pair them off for drill." Raising his eyes to the sun layering with dark clouders, he announced, "We're going to shorten sail, Lieutenant."

"Aye, aye, sir."

Horne climbed the ladder to the quarterdeck, leaning against the taffrail as the prisoners paired off with the seamen. Arms folded against his chest, he watched closely to see which hands tried to avoid mingling with the new men and which prisoners kept back from being coupled with the crew.

The *Eclipse* was tilting more wildly with the increasing wind, masts and spars dipping from side-to-side, making a climb into the shrouds dangerous. But a ship's safety came first, even taking precedence over the life of the crew.

The men on the flying jib let go of the halyards. Keeping the sheet fast, they allowed the sail to run down the stay, letting the wind escape from the upper half. With a shout from the men, the sheet was released, and the wind quickly puffed out from the lower half, making the haul easy and quick.

Horne moved his eyes aft, seeing the two prisoners, Groot and Kiro, tackling the royals; the Dutch and Japanese prisoners held the weather sheet fast for the wind to go out of the canvas, tugging in unison on the weather clemline to haul it down. Neither Groot nor Kiro were big men but Horne could see that they were both putting all their strength into their work.

Leaning back to study the topgallant, he listened to the familiar shouts of 'Haul taut' . . . 'lower away' . . . 'haul down' . . . Squinting his eyes, he watched the African thief, Jud Mwambi, move aloft with the agility of an experienced hand. Horne hoped all the prisoners would show as much skill with muskets and knives as they showed as seamen.

Another call caught Horne's attention, a shout from the masthead.

"Sail ho!"

Horne looked by habit to starboard.

"Sail ho," hailed the mainmast. "To larboard bow."

Turning to his left, Horne pulled a spyglass from the pocket of his new frock coat and trained it on the stretch of cliffs and distant mountains of the Indian shoreline known as the Malabar Coast.

The mainmast hailed, "Native craft, ahoy! Double mast and sweeps."

The *Eclipse* dipped deeply from the swells. Horne could not fix the vessel in his spyglass but he guessed that a two-masted craft with oars could only be a pattimar, one of the Indian vessels which travelled the Malabar Coast. They were six hours south of Bombay and, as local traders would not be venturing seaward in a brewing storm, he suspected that the ship was probably a prowling coastal pirate.

5

"Clear for Action"

Adam Horne sighted his spyglass on the two-masted pattimar plunging towards the *Eclipse*. He could not spot a flag or pennant of allegiance run up its mast. Although he had no wish to fire upon a friendly trader's ship, neither did he want to be taken unawares by one of the many raiders infesting the coves and inlets of the Malabar Coast. Polygars lived in the hills from Kolhapur to Quilian and kept small fleets to rob merchant traffic. There was always danger, too, from Tamil pirates who rounded Cape Comorin from the Coromandel Coast, preying upon ships for rich cargo and valuable weapons.

Estimating the amount of time before the unidentified vessel would be within firing range, Horne took a quick inventory of his cannon power. The *Eclipse* was rated at thirty-four guns, having twenty-six twelve pounders on the main deck, four six pounders on the quarterdeck, and four nine pounders, as well as four swivel guns, on the forecastle.

With time to run out the guns for battle, he wanted to make certain that all members of the crew had eaten before they engaged in what could possibly become an extended encounter.

"Pilkington, have all the men been fed?"

"Aye, aye, sir," came the reply.

Pleased that the *Eclipse* would not have to lose time whilst the crew went to the galley, Horne called for all fires aboard to be extinguished, then ordered, "Have the decks sanded, Lieutenant, larboard and starboard, but don't run out the guns yet. We're not the aggressor."

He trained his spyglass back towards the jagged shoreline. The white speck was growing larger against the grey sea, still set on a course straight for the *Eclipse*. Moving the glass across the choppy water to his left, he swept it in the opposite direction. There was no other ship in sight.

Snapping shut the spyglass, Horne began to feel agitated; he was impatient with the vessel for still raising no flag of allegiance, leaving the *Eclipse* waiting to learn if she was being approached by friend or foe. The brewing storm troubled him, too. Governor Spencer already begrudged him the four weeks to discipline and train his sixteen prisoners; a change in weather could slow the voyage to Bull Island and lose him valuable time.

Shouts and the sound of scuffling near the larboard gun-ports disturbed Horne. He turned, ready to discipline any man daring to waste these important moments in a squabble.

Midshipman Bruce waved his musket excitedly, his round cheeks flushed with excitement. "Men overboard! Men overboard!"

Horne descended the ladder three rungs at a time, wondering if one of the seasick prisoners had slipped on the tossing deck. Or perhaps someone had taken advantage of battle preparations and dived overboard in the hope of swimming to the distant shore. This reminded him that he had forgotten to ask if the prisoners could swim when he had selected them from the cells. Few sailors knew how to swim and he might need swimmers in the mission to Fort St. George.

Horne's anger turned on himself. What other omission had he made in choosing these men?

Pilkington stood in front of the larboard nettings. "The Arab and the Britisher with the pigtail, sir. They were rolling the nettings. I turned my back and they leaped up on the railing and jumped feet first into the water."

Horne looked over the railing, down past the bulwark, and saw two men clawing furiously at the white-capped waves. He could not tell which was Eid the Omani and which was Ted Malloy from Bristol; all he could see was two figures far below him in the churning sea.

The sounds of another scuffle alongside him made him glance over his shoulder, in time to see Bapu, the Rajasthani bandit, struggling with Midshipman Bruce and grabbing Bruce's flintlock.

Pilkington moved to stop Bapu, but Horne held him back. "No, let the man be, Lieutenant."

The command surprised Pilkington. "But, sir . . ."

Horne was adamant. "I gave orders to stop any man trying to escape."

"But, sir! That . . . man's disarmed an officer!"

"How else is he to get a weapon?"

"But, sir . . ."

Horne thrust a finger at the sea. "Lieutenant, if those two men reach shore, this prisoner and all thirteen others will be sent back to Bombay Castle . . ."

A loud blast silenced Horne.

Turning, he saw Bapu holding a spent flintlock smoking in one hand, and looking back to the sea, he saw blood colouring the waves and only one man floundering in the choppy water.

Bapu was an excellent marksman, Horne at least was pleased to see that; he beckoned Tyson Lovett to step forward from the Marine rank. Taking the musket from Tyson's hands, he passed it to Bapu who accepted the weapon and knowledgeably checked its muzzle, charge and cap.

"Captain Horne, look!" Midshipman Bruce pointed towards the single swimmer.

Horne glanced back to the sea and recognized the fins of predatory fish.

The one remaining swimmer had also spotted sharks encircling him and he began shouting, waving to be rescued.

"Sir, the man's calling for help." Midshipman Bruce looked to the ship's lifelines and back to Adam Horne.

Horne remained silent, his square jaw working as he

watched the swimmer floundering in the tossing sea. He looked at Bapu standing alongside him, sighting the musket towards the water.

Bruce became more eager to help the shouting swimmer. "Sir, shall I toss him the lifeline?"

Pilkington was also beginning to show concern. "There's not much time left, sir."

Horne kept his eyes on the swimmer. He already knew the command he would give. He paused only to curse some meddling voice nagging inside him to spare the swimmer's life, to be forgiving or show mercy, a sentimental conscience which totally disregarded the mission's success.

His voice low and steady, Horne ordered, "Fire."

The musket ball struck its target. The swimmer's head exploded into fragments as if it had been a melon bobbing in the surf. The sharks dived at the fresh splash of scarlet.

Bapu lowered the musket's barrel and handed it to Horne.

Horne took the musket and passed it back to Tyson Lovett, knowing many men aboard the *Eclipse* were scandalized by his orders, but also remembering the man who had obeyed them. He looked at Bapu and acknowledged him with a nod, a small reward for fine service. He hoped it would not be the big Asian's one and only show of loyalty.

Behind Horne, Pilkington and Bruce stood at the railing, their faces pale, their eyes flinching. The swimmer had disappeared under the water, all traces of blood diluting in the waves.

Pulling the spyglass from his pocket, Horne trained

it on the approaching vessel and saw a blue puff of cannon smoke drift up past its raked foresail. Kolhapur or Tamil, the unmarked ship had finally shown its intentions.

Horne snapped shut the spyglass. Ah! There was no conscience now about retaliation!

"Clear for action!"

The pattimar was sailing on the opposite tack towards the *Eclipse*, struggling up to windward.

Horne ordered, "Steer small."

Tandimmer, hearing the command, understood Adam Horne's intention without needing a further explanation; soon the *Eclipse* lay in front of the gale, the sea crashing and foaming around her, the rigging creaking as if it might snap from the force, while the rising wind served as auxiliary power to the shortened sails.

Adam Horne's distress about ordering the deaths of two men had disappeared for the moment; the first stage of battle demanded his attention.

"Sir, do you think they're raiders?"

Horne did not answer Pilkington's question; he was thinking about the enemy's manoeuvres.

"Do you think, sir, they'll fire again at such long range?"

The *Eclipse* had not yet opened fire and the worst moment of battle was the wait to send the first volley. But Horne had learnt years ago that the best element of defence in any battle was timing, knowing how to fire at the most opportune moment.

Pilkington glanced at the sand spread to keep the

gunners from sliding on deck. "Guns ready, sir."

Horne remained patient, responding almost pater-
nally to Pilkington despite the fact that the First Lieutenant was three years his senior.

"Lieutenant, we must not form our action on enemy
fire. They could only be trying to draw us out."

Pilkington frequently asked a younger man's questions, especially when he was excited or stressed.

"Draw out, sir?"

"Yes, Lieutenant. The enemy captain might claim
later that he shot a distress signal and that we opened
fire against him."

"Who would he tell that to, sir?"

"Raiders along the Malabar Coast have been known
to sell their allegiance to the French, Lieutenant.
France pays a good price to get allies near Bombay. A
careless incident here on the Malabar Coast could dis-
tract attention from the Navy's blockade in the Bay of
Bengal."

"Yes, sir. Of course, sir." Pilkington often forgot that
his Captain had a mind for diplomacy.

Horne studied the approaching vessel again through
the spyglass, trying to estimate at what angle the two
ships would meet if they continued on the present
course, and which vessel would be windward, the
Eclipse or the pattimar.

Snapping shut the spyglass, he asked, "Merlin on the
portside guns?"

"Aye, aye, sir."

"Canister on top of round shot?"

"Aye, aye, sir."

"See that the matches are lit in the buckets, Lieutenant. There's wash over the bulwark and one wave would ruin an entire round of shot."

Pilkington returned to Horne's side as another blue puff rose from the pattimar's snubbed prow.

Horne studied the enemy with his naked eye. "She fired again."

"Yes, sir. I see the smoke, sir. But I didn't see the ball splash in the water."

Horne looked through the spyglass for any sign of flag or pennant but still saw nothing, not even the flash of insignia, the glint of the sun on a good luck charm painted on the prow.

A third puff of cannon smoke rose from the enemy ship. Pilkington pointed as the sound of a ball came sizzling across the waves, crashing below the water line of the *Eclipse*.

"Strike, sir," cried Pilkington.

Horne ignored the hit. It was time to put into effect the first part of his plan.

"Put helm a'weather," he shouted to the Sailing Master. "And hold, Tandimmer."

George Tandimmer guessed how Adam Horne had decided to deal with the enemy. He smiled at him for taking daredevil chances.

To Pilkington, Horne ordered, "Starboard prepare to fire."

"Aye, aye, sir." Pilkington was galvanized by Horne's orders for action.

Horne listened to the effect of Tandimmer's work—the groan of the wheel, the extra boost given by the wind to the ship's turn. If the enemy continued to behave as he expected, each round of canister shot could pepper the pattimar with two hundred musket balls.

The enemy continued to advance exactly as Horne had predicted: the pattimar had seen the *Eclipse*'s change of tack and was immediately following suit, plunging against the wind. As he had also suspected, the driving winds placed the native craft in a helpless position in front of the *Eclipse*, its oars raised, reminding Horne of the wings of a pigeon in flight, exposing a tender breast to be shot by the hunter—the frigate's starboard guns.

"Fire!"

The frigate rumbled.

A broadside strike on the pattimar brought a cheer from the crew. But Horne ignored the success, concentrating on how to keep a full move ahead of the enemy.

Cupping his hands to his mouth, he shouted, "Stand by to go about!"

The wind was fierce, tossing waves across deck, but the *Eclipse* had the benefit of the gauge and of a crew used to an unpredictable captain. The hands grabbed eagerly at the sheets, tugging haul lines before the pattimar had the opportunity to recover from the first blast, giving the frigate the advantage of the next attack.

"Fire!"

The second bombardment struck the pattimar's stern.

The crew aboard the *Eclipse* was wild now with excitement, but Horne remained silent on the quarterdeck, his weathered face immobile, the creases deep around his eyes, his jaw working as he wondered whether the pattimar captain had realized that the *Eclipse* would soon lose the benefit of the gale.

Deciding to strike whilst he still had the position, he again cupped both hands to his mouth. "Fire!"

The gun crew, crouching with red bandanas knotted around their heads to save their eardrums from the cannon roar, saw the gunner captain, Dick Merlin, chop down his arm for them to proceed as he also shouted, "Fire, you bloody buggers! Fire!"

The burst from the *Eclipse*'s cannons was matched by a burst of flame from the pattimar's guns. Both vessels shuddered from the strikes.

Horne felt the deck tremble beneath his feet. He heard cries from amidship. The enemy had hit men, but he had no time to think about injuries or deaths.

Deciding to change tack and fire on the enemy leeward, he halted the command when he saw the pattimar beginning to swing about, its snub nose turning towards the headland.

Horne raised his spyglass. Was the pattimar retreating?

The frigate's gun crew, interpreting the enemy's flight as their victory, pulled off their bandanas and cheered.

Lieutenant Pilkington, also interpreting the fleeing ship as a victory, rejoiced, "We bettered them, Sir! We bettered them!"

Horne remained silent, gripping one fist in front of his chest as he watched the pattimar retreating for the coastline, the choppy waves licking at her stern.

Pilkington noticed Horne's reservation. His own excitement faded. "Didn't we better them, sir?"

Horne did not reply; he suspected that the enemy had a plan of his own.

A call from the masthead confirmed Horne's suspicions.

"Sails, ho! One to starboard! Second to larboard! Sails ho!"

Horne snapped open the spyglass. He instantly spotted the first white speck moving from the headland. He turned to his right and saw the tilting sail of another ship.

Two more ships were joining the pattimar. The enemy had manoeuvred the *Eclipse* into a trap.

6

Angria's Reef

The two enemy vessels moved to the north and south
of the first unidentified ship, holding the *Eclipse* in the
direct path of a westerly gale and leaving a channel for
the frigate to dash towards the coastline.

The storm was worsening. Jagged streaks of lightning cut the sky. Huge rollers bombarded the frigate,
lifting her with a violent force and dropping the hull
with a loud crash against the thrashing sea. Horne ordered blocks to be placed beneath the trucks of the
cannons to prevent them from breaking loose and ca-
reering across deck; he had the water casks secured
below deck and found time to visit the wardroom
cabin, having a few words with the wounded. Through
all the stowing and battening and words of encourage-
ment, his mind was on the three enemy ships hove to
like snob-nosed sea vultures in the storm. What were
they planning? Were they waiting for the *Eclipse* to
make a lunge for the shore? Why?

Local seamen would know every little inlet and current of the Malabar Coast, giving them an advantage over the *Eclipse*. Adam Horne paced the quarterdeck in the pelting rain, telling himself that he was cowardly to credit the enemy with knowledge he did not possess. He was merely providing himself with an excuse for his own inadequacies, for his own shortcomings as a navigator.

Horne's training in the Bombay Marine had included preparing maps for the Company and studying charts passed down by former captains and pilots, some maps old enough to have been drawn upon leather, the later ones detailed upon vellum.

He did not notice a figure, hunched against the storm, approaching him on the quarterdeck. He continued pacing out his irritation, trying to picture the coastline in his brain, and he walked abruptly into Lieutenant Pilkington.

Rain dripping from his face, Pilkington leaned closer to Horne and shouted over the wind, "Sir, I brought you covering."

Ignoring the coat which Pilkington offered him, Horne continued weighing the idea which had occurred to him: a possible answer to his present dilemma and at least one reason for the behaviour of the three enemy ships.

He looked into Pilkington's rain-covered face. "The answer's on the chart."

Pilkington leaned his head closer to hear.

"Bull's charts!" shouted Horne. "Our answer's on the charts drawn by Commodore Bull!"

Pilkington shook his head. He did not understand what Horne meant.

"The answer!" Horne pointed ashore.

Seeing confusion on Pilkington's face, he realized it was futile to try to explain himself in a howling gale.

"I want to see you in my cabin," he shouted. "*My cabin!*"

Pilkington nodded to show he understood.

Horne remembered that the quartermaster, Jim Striker, had replaced George Tandimmer at the wheel.

"You. Tandimmer. Merlin. And Rajit. I want to see the four of you in my cabin." He held up four fingers. "*Four!*"

Pilkington managed a salute. He turned, bracing himself against the gale, and moved towards the ladder.

A roller smashed over the taffrail. Pilkington stopped, steadying himself in its wash, and continued towards the ladder. Horne followed in Pilkington's wake.

At the foot of the companionway Horne shed his dripping frock coat and cocked hat. He pushed open the door of his cabin, stowing the sodden objects in the nearest locker and grabbed the first item he found in a sea chest to use as a towel.

Moving towards the teak chart case as he rubbed his face and hair, he looked through the racks, finding the chart marked "Panaji Bank."

Enough light poured through the stern windows for him to read the vellum map spread on his desk. He did not raise his eyes from the indigo markings as he called for Pilkington and the other three men to enter the cabin.

"That's the reason right there." Horne stabbed his finger at the chart. "They're wreckers."

The four men looked from Horne down to the chart, and a silence fell over the cabin.

Pilkington spoke first. "Wreckers, sir?"

"A trap I should have expected." Horne resumed drying his hair.

Pilkington bent over the desk, careful not to drip any rainwater on the chart.

Horne pointed towards the coastline. "See. By those tide markings. There's a bank."

Confused, Pilkington raised his eyes from the chart. A few minutes ago, Horne had been pacing the quarterdeck in the storm, carrying the weight of the world on his shoulders. Now he was enthusiastic, confident, a completely different man.

George Tandimmer looked to where Horne's finger pointed on the chart. "Angria's Reef."

Horne nodded, shooting a conspiratorial glance at his Sailing Master.

Pilkington's voice was cautious. "A reef stands between us and the coastline?"

Horne's excitement was growing. "Yes. There's been a drift and we're dead off what's called Angria's Reef. We usually make east of it. But whoever those pirates are, they lured us towards the coastline."

Pausing, Horne looked down and saw that he was using his new silk shirt for a towel.

The four men waited for him to continue.

Horne tossed the shirt into a corner. "We're trapped.

North and south. With Angria's Reef between us and shore."

Dick Merlin's ruddy face tightened with anger. "So that bloody pop-gun fight was nothing but a trick to lure us off course."

Horne looked at his gun captain. "That's right, Merlin. They have us exactly where they want us."

"But they caught some of our fire, sir." Merlin looked from Horne to Pilkington and Rajit. "They took two broadsides and a blast right up their arse. We can at least grin at that, can't we?"

Horne saw no reason to give any unrealistic hopes. "They'll be the ones grinning, Merlin, when they gather our cannons from the wreckage on the reef."

Tandimmer moved forward. "Sir, should we forget about . . ." He tapped the vellum, ". . . here?"

Horne remained silent, keeping his eyes on Pilkington, Merlin and Rajit as they bent over the desk to study the point on the chart at which Tandimmer was pointing. Horne was pleased that at least one of his men had realized this possibility for movement.

Pilkington looked from the map to Horne. He understood Tandimmer's suggestion but disagreed. "Sir, that's open sea! The storm's from the west. That could be worse than the reef!"

Horne shook his head. "At least we have a chance there, Lieutenant."

"But the gale, sir." Pilkington looked to Merlin and Rajit for support. "The wind could drive us straight onto the reef."

"Possibly, Lieutenant. But we have a better chance of escape if we beat to windward, trying to make board by board. The going will be slow and tedious. But we must try to make headway."

He scanned the faces of his men for their reaction. Pilkington's thin eyebrows were knit, obviously still unconvinced by the plan. Merlin remained red with rage at the wreckers. Rajit showed no opinion one way or other, a true soldier. Tandimmer's freckled face beamed with the possibility of tackling the challenge.

"We have no time to lose, men. We must all work in unison." Horne looked at Rajit. "Sergeant, detail the prisoners to the bilge pumps for the next watch."

Rajit stiffened to attention.

"All prisoners except for three, Sergeant. Leave Groot the Dutchman and Kiro the Japanese for the jib. And Jud the African for up top."

"Suh!"

Horne turned to the gunner. "Merlin, I want the blocks checked under all the trucks. We don't need to be chasing twelve-pounders in a storm."

"Aye, aye, sir."

Dismissing Rajit and Merlin, he opened a desk drawer for a flint light. The storm had worsened in the past few minutes, darkening the sky and making a lantern necessary for Pilkington, Tandimmer and himself to be able to study the chart and plot a path to safety.

The Arabian Sea thundered against the *Eclipse*; steep waves lifted the frigate, tilting her at an incline, and dropped the bow down through the rollers, letting the stern crash into a trough.

Adam Horne worked with George Tandimmer on the first steps of their plan, tying two helmsmen to the wheel for the men's safety in the storm, and to hold the westerly course charted away from the coastline.

Waves swept the decks as the ship rocked side to side, creeping forward board-by-board into the storm under short sail.

The topsman came down from the main mast and, finding Horne in the protection of the forecastle, reported that Jud, the African prisoner, was following him down from the top gallant.

Horne sent the topsman below deck to eat supper. Wrapping an oilskin coat tighter around himself, he stepped out from the overhang and tried to spot Jud in the foaming crash of waves.

Satisfaction from guessing the enemy's trap had abandoned him. He was remembering that two of the sixteen prison recruits were dead. In the chilling, wet face of the storm's turbulence, he realized more than ever how undermanned the *Eclipse* was. He felt a mixture of revulsion at having to waste two human lives and a selfish, cold-hearted outrage at losing valuable manpower for his mission.

Squinting his eyes against the whipping spray, Horne studied the snapping ratlines for the movement of the African prisoner. He did not want to lose another man.

Lightning flashed across the sky, making the masts and shrouds flicker in the pattern of spider-webbing against the storm. But there was no sign of Jud.

Stepping back to the protection of the forecastle, Horne shed the long tarpaulin coat and began pulling off his leathered-soled boots. Bare-footed, he moved cautiously across the canting deck, reaching the

weather foremost shroud, and jumped to grab the ratlines. He climbed hand-over-hand in the biting rain,
swinging back and forth in the gale, until he reached
the lubber's hole.

While the wind pasted his clothes to his body, he
swung to the futtock shroud and, hanging backwards
from the ropes, continued his climb until he reached
the fore top gallant yardarm. Then, steadying himself
on the cross tree, he squinted through the driving wind.
Jud was stretched a few feet away from him on the
yardarm.

The African lay face downwards, clinging with both
arms to the yardarm, the pink soles of his bare feet
facing Horne.

The storm was tossing the ship's masts in a circle,
dipping Jud downwards as the ship tilted to larboard,
rushing him backwards into a momentary upright position as she heaved to starboard, his face turned to the
sky, then crashing his head back down to the sea.

A bowline had tangled around Jud's ankle, and
Horne saw that the African could not free himself without releasing his hold.

Falling belly down on the yardarm, Horne eased
himself out towards Jud, using his knees to propel himself, and gradually pulling himself along with his
hands. His fingers soon located the cause of the trouble. Rain and wind had tightened the bowline and knotted it firmly around Jud's ankle.

Pulling and working at the soaked line with one
hand, Horne's fingers soon tired and he switched to the
other hand. The frigate dipped and rose continuously,

the storm blowing as if to wrench Horne and Jud from their roost.

Horne finally freed a knot by loosening a gasket holding the bowline and pulled it from the line, so allowing Jud to loosen the rest of the rope with quick jerks of the ankle. He hurried back towards the cross tree and made room for Jud to follow.

Jud tried his ankle in a few cautionary twists, grinned his gratitude at Horne over his shoulder and scooted in from the yardarm.

Horne gestured to Jud to lead the way back down to deck.

A wave crested as Jud reached the futtock shroud, Horne following a short distance behind. Jud cleared the lubber's hole but Horne waited until the wash of the next wave exploded with a loud crash and diminished into foam.

Continuing downward, Horne halted occasionally on the slippery ratlines as the gale thrashed him back and forth. Resuming his hand-under-hand descent, he stepped into mid-air with his left foot, felt his right foot slipping on the rope, and the next thing he knew his hand could not find support, and he was falling.

African spirits came through ancestors. But as Jud had never known his parents he prayed instead to the spirit of his dead son, asking the boy to help him save this Englishman who had risked his life rescuing him.

Adam Horne's motionless body lay heavy on Jud's back as he inched his way across the canting deck from the spot where Horne had fallen from the ratlines.

The waves crashed over the bulwark, washing the

deck. Jud paused in the foamy wake, begging his dead son to give him strength to reach the hatch, then continued crawling on his hands and knees towards the coaming.

Jud's son had died in childbirth at Sheik All Hadd's Castle of the Golden Sand, the fortress in Oman where Jud's Nubian wife, Maringa, had been a household slave.

Carrying Horne on his back, Jud promised his son that, if this ship reached Bull Island, he would work hard to prove himself a good man, a strong man, to make amends for having turned to crime after Maringa had died.

7

A Bad Dream

The **Eclipse** *lay* before the gale, the sea smothering her
decks with iron-black waves as jagged spears of lightning cracked open the sky. The crash of water and
thunder was cut by a rasp of rock tearing wood, beginning at the ship's bow, shaking the frigate . . . shaking it . . . shaking it . . .

"Captain sahib! Captain sahib! Wake up, Captain sahib! You're having a bad dream!"

Adam Horne sat bolt upright in bed. He stared at a
young turbanned Asian shaking him by the shoulder.

"Captain sahib, you fell and hit your head. You sleep
and sleep and then you have, oh such bad dreams. Captain sahib."

Horne focused his eyes more clearly and recognized
the small, neatly groomed Indian as the prisoner, Jingee, the young dubash who had stabbed an Englishman
to death for blaspheming Hindi caste system. Looking

round, he saw a food tray on the brass-bound sea chest next to his bed.

Jingee began straightening the rumpled bed sheets. "I boiled you tea, Captain sahib. I cooked you cakes. *Moong dal*. Very good for you."

Horne pushed Jingee aside. "I can't lie here sipping tea and eating cakes in a storm, boy."

"The storm's over, Captain sahib." Jingee lifted a corner of the thin mattress. "We passed through the storm last night."

Naked, Horne paused, half-out of the narrow bed. Jingee continued tucking at the foot of the mattress. Horne glanced from Jingee to the stern windows. He noticed for the first time that sunshine poured through the mullioned panes, filling the cabin with bright, golden light.

"We sailed far, far south while you slept, Captain sahib."

Horne's hair was tousled from bed but his eyes were alert and quick, the eyes of a man unfamiliar with his bearings.

He looked back to Jingee. "How long have I been asleep?"

"Ten, twelve hours." Jingee shrugged. "Do not worry, Captain sahib. Mr. Tin Hammer comes every two hours to see if you are awake. Mr. Tin Hammer says everything—ship shape."

"Mr . . . who?"

"Tin Hammer."

Horne was more confused. He remembered climbing the shrouds to the yardarm. He remembered untying the knot from Jud's ankle. He had followed Jud down to deck but had fallen on the ratlines. He had obviously hit his head and lost consciousness. But what had happened since then? And who was "Tin Hammer"?

Jingee bunched the tips of his small brown fingers together and beat them against both cheeks, explaining, "Mr. Tin Hammer. The man with oh so many little red dots all over his face."

"*Tan*dimmer."

Jingee nodded. "Him."

Horne moved back under the sheet, momentarily reassured by the mention of familiar, trustworthy people.

"Those dots are called freckles, Jingee and . . ."

Horne paused. What was he doing lying here in bed, taking another man's word for the safety of his ship?

Jingee picked up the food tray from the chest and placed it on Horne's lap. "Eat while it's hot, Captain sahib. You need food."

Horne's first instinct was to push aside the tray and go up on deck. But the food smells were tempting and, telling himself that the *Eclipse* did not seem to be in peril, he broke off a chunk from the warm wheel of cake.

He gobbled it down and broke off a second piece. It was like a pancake—bread—and he realised fleetingly how narrow-minded he had been in not eating Indian food when he was ashore.

He reached for the steaming cup. "Hmmm. Orange tea. Delicious."

Jingee beamed with pride, steepling the flats of both hands together and bowing. "Thank you, Captain sahib. I hope this is better than the food from the galley."

Horne chose to ignore this prim little convict's criticism of the ship's provisions. He broke off another piece of warm cake as he looked around his cabin.

The leather envelopes and the ship's bound ledgers were neatly arranged on his desk. The wooden boxes and wicker hampers were stacked in orderly fashion under the stern window. The carpet had been brushed and lay neatly on a gleaming deck.

Jingee stood quietly alongside the bed as Horne evaluated the condition of the cabin. "I cleaned for you, Captain sahib. But I opened no lockers or chests without your permission."

Horne was suspicious of people trying to organize his living habits. He had only considered allowing one person to become so close to him and that had been Isabel.

"Quite right, Jingee."

"I found these, Captain sahib. I tried to dry them but . . ."

Jingee produced two shapeless objects. One was large, the other small, and he held them with the tips of his fingers as if he were frightened of them.

Horne studied the two objects before recognizing his new frock coat and hat—sodden, limp, ruined. Cursing his stupidity for wearing the new uniform in a storm, he broke off another chunk of bread and, as he began chewing, asked, "Can you try drying them again, Jingee?"

"Yes, Captain sahib."

Like the dutiful dubash Jingee had been trained to be, he continued his report. "Captain sahib, the man called Mr. Flannery says he's a surgeon and comes often to examine you in the cabin. But I tell him you need sleep more than him poking at your head. I do not let Mr. Flannery disturb you, Captain sahib."

"Quite right." Horne had smelled liquor on Flannery's breath when he had last spoken to him.

The cabin—the ship—seemed to be in good order. The sounds of footsteps creaked overhead as the officer of the watch paced the quarterdeck. The call of men's voices rose with the singing of the shrouds and the creak of timber. A familiar sound of pumps rose from the bilges.

Horne started the second bread wheel. "Tell me, Jingee, what are you doing out of the bilges and here taking care of me?"

Jingee bowed, palms together. "The African man who goes up the masts. He brought you down to the bilges after your fall, Captain sahib."

"Jud carried me?"

"Yes, Captain sahib. You were unconscious."

"Jud carried me all the way down to the bilges?"

"That was the only place aboard ship, Captain sahib, you allowed us prisoners to go."

Horne realised that Jud had returned the favour, and had ended up by saving his life.

Jingee continued. "I am no sailor, Captain sahib, but I know something about ships and the wise men who sail them. So I told everybody in the bilges that Captain sahib must not be brought to no go-down. I told everybody that it's only proper for Captain sahib to be in his private cabin. Mr. Tin Hammer says I am right. I helped bring you here with Mr. Tin Hammer."

"Tandimmer," corrected Horne.

Jingee bowed. "Lieutenant Pilkington, too."

"Jingee, you can say Pilkington. So say—Tandim-mer."

"Tod—"

"No. Tan—dim—mer."

"Tad—diu—"

Horne paused. "Tell me about Pilkington, Jingee."

"Lieutenant Pilkington has all the men out in the sunshine, Captain sahib. He calls for 'all hands on deck.' "

Horne was pleased that Pilkington was pursuing his orders to mix the new men with the crew.

Listening again to the voices on deck, he stretched his arms and yawned. "I'll go and make an appearance on deck. Let everybody see I'm still kicking."

"Still 'kicking,' Captain sahib?"

"Still alive." Horne had not felt so rested for as long as he could remember. And perhaps had he found someone to replace Geoff Wheeler, his last steward?

"Captain sahib. You eat. You rest. You get more well."

Horne ignored Jingee. He was listening to the men's voices growing louder on deck.

Realising he was hearing the sounds of men fighting, he shoved aside the food tray and sprang from the bed. He threw open the top of his sea chest and grabbed the first pair of trousers he found. Then he pulled open the cabin door, dashed up the companionway, and pushed his way through the crush of shouting men at the base of the mainmast.

The men surrounded two fighters, the sound of striking fists coming from inside the circle.

Lieutenant Pilkington and Sergeant Rajit were trying

to impose order on the men, swinging cudgels and the butts of their flintlocks. Pilkington grabbed a half-naked man by his bare shoulder but dropped his hand when he realised the identity of the man.

"Captain Horne!"

"Lieutenant, what's going on here?"

By now Sergeant Rajit had also noticed Horne, half-naked and bare-footed, standing on deck. Gradually more men saw Horne amongst them and the circle opened, exposing the fighters.

Horne espied Tom Gibbons, the ginger-whiskered boatswain, with a puffed eye and cut jaw. The prisoner Kevin McFiddich stood next to Gibbons, his lip bleeding and one eye badly cut.

A voice shouted, "Those prison rats started it, Captain!"

"Lying coward!" shouted a prisoner.

Another seaman bellowed, "Go back to the hole you crawled out of!"

As the men began hurling insults at one another, Gibbons and McFiddich flung themselves back into their fight, and the circle tightened back around them. Horne's demand for order was lost in the shouts. Pushing into the crowd, he shoved them aside to reach the middle of the circle, catching a fist on his chin and blows on the arm, back and shoulders, before he reached the centre. He shoved Gibbons to one side and stopped McFiddich with a fist.

McFiddich held the bridge of his nose and glared at Horne. "Why hit me? Protecting your favourites?"

Horne's fist flew at him again.

As McFiddich stumbled back on the deck, the crew cheered.

Horne turned on his men. "What kind of bloody animals are you?"

Looking towards Pilkington, he shouted, "Lieutenant, I want an explanation for this behaviour."

Pilkington stepped forward. "Sir, we were pulling down the netting for drills when—"

A voice interrupted. "These pigs want us to do their work for them."

Horne spun around and saw the Spanish prisoner, Fernando Vega. He grabbed the Spaniard by the bicep and slapped him across the face. "Never interrupt me."

He pushed Vega back towards the crowd and, facing the men, shouted, "Nobody fights unless I say 'fight!' Understand?"

He thumbed his chest. "If you want to pick a fight with somebody, pick it with me."

He stepped towards McFiddich who was hunched on deck. "You want to fight, McFiddich?"

McFiddich did not raise his head.

Horne kicked at him. "I'm talking to you, McFiddich."

McFiddich lifted his glowering eyes up the length of Horne's body.

"Go on, McFiddich," taunted Horne. "Go on. Prove what a man you are."

McFiddich held Horne's angry glare.

"What's the matter, McFiddich, you a coward?"

"Don't push me—"

Horne stepped back, leaning forward from his waist

and beckoning to McFiddich. "Come on, coward. Come on—"

McFiddich lunged for him.

Horne stepped aside, cutting down his right hand onto McFiddich's neck and driving him down to deck. He drove the heel of his foot between McFiddich's shoulder blades, pulled back his other foot and repeated a tattoo of sharp kicks into the man's kidneys.

He turned to Tom Gibbons. "What about you, Gibbons? You want to fight me too?"

The ginger-haired boatswain backed away from Horne, shaking his head. "Sir, you didn't do nothing to me. I got no gripe—"

"Then why don't I *do* something to you, Gibbons? Why don't I—"

Horne widened the knuckles of his second and third fingers, reaching to twist the end of Gibbons' nose. "Why don't I do . . . *this*?"

His other hand flew up and grabbed Gibbons' mutton-chop whiskers.

"Or this? Or—"

Horne slugged Gibbons in the stomach, wrapped an arm around the boatswain and locked him helplessly to his side.

"Now listen to me, Gibbons, and listen hard. No matter who does what to you on this ship, you ignore him. Understand?"

He drove his fist into Gibbons' ribs. "Understand?"

"Yes—"

"Yes who?"

"Yes, sir."

"That's right, Gibbons. You're learning, Gibbons. And this is to make you remember."

Horne drove his fist a second time into Gibbons' ribs. He released him from his grip, shoving him towards deck.

Turning to face the crew, prisoners and Marines, he spoke in a low even voice, his hazel eyes wild with excitement, sharp with anger.

"I tried to be fair with you men. I tried to treat you decently. Now I see that I was wrong. I see you're the kind of men who have to learn the hard way. So I'm going to teach you the hard way.

"Whether you like it or not, you're all part of this ship. Understand? And as you're part of this ship, you're also going to be part of Bull Island. The sooner you start realising that fact, the less trouble you're going to get from me.

"But the one thing you can count on from here is that I'm going to teach you the hard way. Every day. Every night. You're going to end up better men than you are now. Or you're going to end up . . . dead. No matter who you are. Ship hands. Marines. Prisoners from Bombay Castle. You'll all be the same."

Nervous coughs passed through the crowd.

"The next man who fights is—" Horne pointed to the sea, "—thrown overboard."

Horne looked at Rajit. "Do you hear that order, Sergeant? The next man who fights is thrown overboard."

Rajit saluted. "Suh!"

"If we're in shallow water, Sergeant, the orders are to tie the man's arms behind him, shoot him in both legs and *then* throw him overboard."

"Suh!"

Horne looked at Gibbons and McFiddich. "As for these two men, Sergeant, lock them in bilboes. They will stay below deck till we make landfall."

"Suh!"

Horne turned to Pilkington. "Lieutenant, I want to see you in my cabin. Midshipman Bruce and Midshipman Mercer will proceed with drill. I also want to see Mr. Flannery and Mr. Tandimmer. And the man over there—Jud."

"Aye, aye, sir."

Remembering a disciplinary order he had already given, he added, "Is Babcock doing his deck duty, Lieutenant?"

"Aye, aye, sir."

Horne glanced at the big-eared Colonial. "Good."

He raised his eyes towards the main royals. There was a southerly wind, but its strength was little more than a breeze. Turning, he padded down the companionway in his bare feet.

The rest of the day passed without incident and, as the sun sank beyond the curving horizon, Tim Flannery emerged from the wardroom cabin and stood by the larboard railing, watching a spectacular suffusion of purple and orange in the far distance of the Arabian Sea. The Malabar Coast had not been sighted for over a day.

Flannery was a rangy man with silky white hair and a network of tiny red veins patterning his round cheeks. He held a tin brandy flask in his bony hands as he leaned on the railing, the sunset reflecting in the blank cast of his eyes.

A voice behind him asked, "Thinking of swimming ashore, doc?"

Flannery turned and saw one of the prisoners from Bombay Castle. Not knowing the man's name or country of origin, Flannery held out his brandy flask as a token of introduction. "Want to come with me, bucko?"

The prisoner, Fred Babcock, took his first greedy drink of brandy for three years.

Handing the flask back to Flannery, he answered, "I've got nowhere to run to, even if I did make it ashore. This spot seems to be as good a place as any for a man to sort out his mind."

"I'd think that a spell in Bombay Prison would've given you time enough to do all the thinking you needed."

Babcock laughed, pulling one of his big ears. "I was sentenced for life. Where was I going? What use did I have for thinking?"

"Bucko, your voice has a twang to it. You an emmigrant from the Americas?"

Babcock nodded proudly. "Ohio Valley. Best bottom land in the world. But I got no home, no kin to go back to even if I could."

"Captain Horne's going to take care of all your problems, bucko. He's going to make a Marine out of you."

"I don't know if I *want* to be some . . . Bombay Marine."

Flannery passed back the flask. "How did you end up in prison, bucko?"

"An officer started pushing me around on a ship out of Boston. He kept pushing and pushing and when I didn't push back, he finally took a swing at me. I defended myself and landed him right smack on his butt. Only trouble was his head hit a capstan and killed him straight out." Babcock upended the flask over his mouth.

Enjoying the deep swallow of liquor, he asked in a brighter voice, "Why're you aboard this tub, doc?"

Flannery reached for the flask and took a long swig. Smacking his thin lips with contentment, he answered, "Revenge."

"Revenge?"

"Sweet, driving, slow-burning revenge."

"Revenge for what, doc?"

Flannery fixed his liquid emerald eyes on the far horizon. "You're the man who wants to sort out his problems, bucko, not me. I've known what I want for the past sixteen years. I'm just not having much luck finding the fancy devil."

Babcock pulled on his ear again. "Sorry to tell you this, doc, but according to what Captain Horne says about this Bull Island place, you ain't going to find much sign of nobody there."

"Revenge, bucko, is like this brandy. It gets sweeter and stronger with each passing year. This ship will leave Bull Island one day and you can be sure as there's a St. Paddy I'll be aboard."

Babcock bit back the urge to say that revenge was also like a mad dog. It turned on you. He suspected that the lanky Irish surgeon might not be a safe man to befriend.

8

Bull Island

Adam Horne greeted Lieutenant Pilkington on the quarterdeck the second morning after the storm. "Lieutenant, I want the lifelines strung today."

Pilkington thought he had misheard the order. The sea was barely ruffled by the breeze.

"I also want six spools of rope brought on deck, Lieutenant."

"Aye, aye, sir." Pilkington descended the ladder.

Horne was in a foul temper this morning. Despite reports that the shot holes had been plugged in the hull, that ripped sails had been replaced or repaired, his mood had remained black for the past two days.

The fight between Gibbons and McFiddich had reminded him how isolated he was aboard the *Eclipse*. Apart from Pilkington, his commissioned officers were few, very junior, and had not as yet shown themselves to be capable of handling a difficult crew. Sergeant Rajit was the only other figure of strength aboard the frigate, but being a Sepoy and a Sergeant, he conscientiously kept his place—well down the line of command.

Horne suspected that his bad mood was caused by more than not having adequate support aboard the *Eclipse*. He was becoming lonely, and this realisation angered him.

The last voyage had been his first mission of consequence as a captain. Isolated in his command, he had begun to understand the fabled loneliness suffered by captains, commanders, any man who had to make decisions and be responsible for the safety of human life. Unlike many commanders, Horne had no family to go home to, no one to confide in except his crew or subordinate officers. These options were pared down as the number of subordinates dwindled each passing month, or as his crew became more surly, more tired, spent in one way or another.

The success of his mission to the North Arabian Sea had become obsessive to him; the prospect of failing, frustrating. Dedication to his command became the focus of his life. He began to feel little different from Indian warriors who drugged themselves for battle, but instead of opium his drug was an incessant personal drive. Secretly, he envied men who kept their work separate from the rest of their lives. But he had no other life except work. Nor did he have any prospect of one. His memory of Isabel was so vivid, so devoted, so painful that he could not even consider offering his hand to anyone else.

Being a practical man, he kept reminding himself that a life in the Bombay Marine was his own choice, that he must pursue it with all his gusto, not question any decisions he made. The path to excellence, however, had its own variety of pitfalls; a man's problems were doubled when his orders were tied to tight schedules.

This morning Horne had awakened realising he was losing valuable time in training a squadron for Fort St. George. The thought had attacked him like some gnawing worm. Washing and shaving, he had decided to start doing something about training the men today. As he dressed, he had wondered if he were beginning to hide again in his work, but he had instantly pushed the question from his mind. He did not want to solve one worry and pass to another, to become obsessed with personal problems, a man who whined, complained, carried his troubles like a flag, some banner of misery to flap every day of his life. Oh, no. The ideal was a decisive one. He had also pondered the idea that it might be advantageous to keep himself from forming personal attachments to other people. Pain and hurt were not only caused by enemy cannon at sea.

Horne stood on the quarterdeck, watching Pilkington ordering the lifelines being strung from starboard to larboard. He descended the ladder to direct the way he wanted the auxiliary ropes laced lengthwise across the lifelines.

Satisfied at last with the weaving of squares, he stripped off his shirt and boots and began to lead Sergeant Rajit, Tyson Lovett and four other men from the Marine unit in a high-legged run through the course created by the ropes. Then organizing a larger group—

a collection of Marines, crew, and prisoners—he ordered the ropes to be raised higher, making the exercise more difficult. For the next course he raised them higher still and invited Sergeant Rajit to join him in leading the drill.

For the following exercise, Horne sent the men beneath the ropes, ordering them to crawl on their bellies, keeping their hips down, propelling themselves by their elbows and shoulders, heads pressed flat to the deck. He called for Sergeant Rajit to stand nearby with a birch rod ready in one hand in case a man raised his back or buttocks.

Before the morning ended, he had evolved the men into four groups, four combinations of crew, prisoners and Marines arranged in graduated degrees of physical stamina, quickness and brute strength.

After the midday meal, he ordered two ropes to be suspended from the top mainmast yardarm and watched the prisoners compete with the crew in a climb. He hoped the contest would release some of the hatred between them. He was not surprised by Jud's excellence in the rope climb. Apart from being strong, the big African seemed to be a friendly, contented man, almost having a religious air to him.

The prisoners all impressed Horne one way or another with their strength. Jingee moved more quickly than Horne had expected. He wondered if the young Tamil dubash would prove to be as gifted in physical agility as he was at cooking and cleaning. The Turk, Mustafa, never smiled but never tired from daybreak to dusk. The Dutch sailor, Groot, was strong, bright, eager to please his new *schupper*.

But the men of the ship's Marine unit greatly disappointed Horne. They lacked stamina, moving sloppily and sluggishly. He remembered, though, that they were tired, having returned from a recent voyage, some of them being far past the retirement age by the standards of the Royal Navy, only acceptable to a force as desperate for manpower as the Bombay Marine.

On the fifth day out of Bombay, the first sight of land was hailed from the mainmast. Horne ordered all men to deck. He sent for Gibbons and McFiddich to be freed from the bilboes for landfall.

Sailing under topsail, the *Eclipse* moved gracefully between large, conical-shaped islands, many covered with vegetation and palms, past smaller islands, some no bigger than a rock protruding from the clear turquoise water.

Horne had studied Bull's chart carefully and was pleased that his calculations for arrival were proving correct. With the yards trimmed for an anchoring course, he saw the water shoaling quickly and estimated they would be dropping anchor within the hour at what had once been the French penal island.

The leadsman called, "By the mark nine . . ."

Horne felt the sun's heat cresting in a cloudless blue sky.

"By the mark eight . . ."

Men lined the rails, waiting to catch the first glimpse of their temporary home.

"By the mark seven . . ."

Horne kept his eyes on a rocky promontory of the island off the larboard bow. "Anchor clear?"

"Aye, aye, sir. Clear."

"By the mark seven . . ."

"Let go anchor."

As the cable coursed through the hawsehole, the watch scrambled to furl the topsails and the *Eclipse* began to swing in her course. The wind played with the ship like a cat toying with a leaf, gently batting the frigate on the flowing tide as the anchor dragged weight.

As the *Eclipse* continued to swing in the wind, an inlet came into sight, the view of a few roofless stone buildings and a rocky shore pocked with salt pans. The men lining the railings stared silently at the stony shoreline, at an island barren except for a few coconut palms and patches of brown grass.

The most prominent structure was a tall gallows jabbing up into the sky, the shred of a hangman's rope tossing in the breeze from the wooden crossbeam.

9

The Three Governors

North-east of the Laccadive Islands, the sun ripened dead fish and rotting fruit in Bombay's noisy harbour. A swarm of *dongis* skimmed across the murky water towards the wharf, the oarsmen playfully shouting *"Ram! Ram! Ram!"* as they passed a lumbering *ulark* loaded with dung cakes. The din of pedlars and fishermen in the waterfront bazaar was cut by the bellow of an elephant, the silver *howdah* on the animal's back decorated with yak tails brightly plaited with ribbons and a myriad of tiny jangling bells. The cacophony and sweetly-spiced stench of the harbour carried up the yellow bastions of Bombay Castle and through the closed shutters of a chamber where Commodore Watson sat in a meeting with the three Governors of the Honourable East India Company.

Commodore Watson's superior, Governor Spencer of Bombay, tall and slim with a neatly trimmed moustache and sharply pointed goatee, sat at the opposite end of a long mahogany table from Governor Vansittart of Bengal who had crossed the subcontinent of India with Governor Pigot of Madras for the meeting at Bombay Castle.

Governor Vansittart was explaining to Commodore Watson the reason why the three Governors had decided to remove the imprisoned French Commander-in-Chief, Thomas Lally, from Fort St. George earlier than scheduled. Slim, elegant, speaking in a mellow voice, he summarized Lally's last year in India.

"Wandewash was the beginning of the end of General Lally. He retreated back to Pondicherry with the British Army at his heels. The Navy joined the Army's siege of Pondicherry in June and, by the end of the year, they had brought Lally to his knees."

Today was the first time Commodore Watson had heard in full why the British Commanders-in-Chief were squabbling amongst themselves over Lally as a prisoner, and why the East India Company planned to interfere—secretly—in the heated dispute.

Vansittart clasped his thin hands on the table as he spoke. "In January, General Lally saw that the French cause was hopeless. He sent an envoy to Colonel Coote, inviting him into the fortress to discuss terms for a formal surrender. Coote accepted the invitation and, whilst he studied the terms of Lally's capitulation, Lally left the fortress and boarded Admiral Pocock's flagship in the harbour. Surrendering a second time to the Navy, Lally submitted documents to Pocock, claiming Pocock—and *dis*claiming Coote—as the one true victor of Pondicherry."

Confused, Watson asked, "Lally double-crossed

Coote? He sneaked out of Pondicherry to Pocock's flagship with a different set of documents?"

Vansittart nodded. "Lally surrendered twice. Once to the Army. A second time to the Navy. Both times excluding the other from the Terms of Capitulation."

Watson was astonished. He looked at Governor Spencer at the head of the table. He glanced across the table at podgy Governor Pigot. "And both officers—distinguished British officers—signed documents excluding the other from a victory?"

Vansittart's slim hands remained folded on the table. "I'm afraid so, Commodore, and the storm which claimed your Marine ships that day proved to be a blessing for Lally's scheme."

"The winds began scattering the British fleet," he went on, "and Admiral Pocock ordered Lally off his flagship. As Pocock hurried to the rescue of the distressed ships, Coote was informed of Lally's disappearance from the fortress. He emerged to find him aboard the Army troop ship. Pleased with his own good luck, Coote struck out through the gale, sailing for Madras where he locked Lally in the Army Guardhouse at Fort St. George and continued north to Calcutta."

Watson expostulated. "How can two British officers allow Lally to . . . manipulate them like this?"

Vansittart reached for a decanter in front of him on the table. Splashing port into a goblet, he replied, "The rightful victor of Pondicherry will not only enjoy a distinguished place in history, Commodore, he will also receive more than sixty thousand pounds in prize money."

The sum of money was a fortune. But Watson was still confused. He looked back at Governor Spencer at the head of the table. "How can this dispute possibly benefit Lally? What's the cad up to?"

Setting down his goblet on the table, Vansittart replied as spokesman for the three Governors. "Lally is most likely trying to buy time to be rescued. We've had reports that d'Ache is gathering the French fleet off Madras."

"Where's Admiral Pocock now?"

"Nearby off the Coromandel Coast. Guarding Madras. Waiting to claim Lally as *his* prize. Making certain that Coote doesn't spirit him off to England."

Watson's head was full of questions. "Why did Coote leave Lally in Madras in the first place?"

Vansittart fingered the goblet's thick stem. "Coote's knee was injured at Wandewash. Originally he was not due to sail back to England until March, so he had time to visit his surgeon in Calcutta. But since then, he's decided to depart at an earlier date. We must act more quickly."

Watson ran a stubby forefinger around the inside of his high-standing collar, hesitating before asking the most difficult of his questions.

"Your Excellency, what does the Company hope to achieve by . . . removing Lally from the Army's Guardhouse and sending him to England? To steal him out from under their noses?"

The answer seemed obvious to Vansittart. "Why, to settle the problem of whose prisoner Lally is. The Army's or the Navy's. We'll deliver Lally to the War

Office in London and settle the dispute once and for all between them."

Watson mopped his bald pate. "But what does the Company hope to achieve for itself? Certainly not prize money?"

Vansittart and Spencer exchanged glances down the length of the mahogany table; they both looked at Governor Pigot sitting between them.

Pigot nodded as his small red hand reached for the decanter in front of him.

Vansittart remained the spokesman. "Commodore Watson, when we deliver Thomas Lally to the War Office in London, we shall submit demands to Sir William Pitt for military control over all regions and territories in which the Company has powers of trade."

It was the honesty that Watson had wanted. But the answer stunned him: the Governors were forming a coalition. Vansittart, Pigot and Spencer were laying the groundwork for an autonomy of Colonial power throughout the Orient!

Looking at Governor Spencer, he rasped, "But what if the mission fails, Your Excellency? What if Captain Horne's squadron doesn't succeed in kidnapping Lally?"

The mellowness disappeared from Vansittart's voice as he answered. "If Captain Horne fails in this mission, Commodore Watson, we shall have no choice but to review the Company's need for maintaining the existence of the Bombay Marine."

Watson dropped both hands to his lap. He did not

want the three Governors to see him trembling.

Vansittart added, "Commodore, we suggest you inform Captain Horne immediately of the change in plans."

PART TWO
The Wheat From
The Chaff

10

The Hard Way

In the three days since dropping anchor off Bull Island, Adam Horne had organized four work groups from the eighty-nine men of the *Eclipse*'s crew, the seventeen Marines of the frigate's fighting unit and the remaining fourteen prisoners recruited from Bombay Castle.

He split the four groups into four shifts of duty: one watch stood guard at all times aboard the *Eclipse*; three sentry posts were stationed around the island; a labour detail repaired buildings and dug latrines; and a drill squad trained from dawn to dusk, breaking only for meals and lessons ranging from tapping cannon with ball and grapeshot to smearing bayonets with goose fat. The four work groups rotated daily in the four divisions of duty.

Lieutenant Pilkington alternated with Midshipman Bruce and Midshipman Mercer in command of ship and shore shifts. Sergeant Rajit headed the drill squads.

Tim Flannery was assigned to a hut on the edge of the island's main cluster of stone buildings and converted it into his infirmary. Horne had also ordered Flannery to shave off the men's hair, beards, and moustaches as a precaution against lice. He offered his own headful of curly chestnut hair as Flannery's first job.

By the fourth morning it was time for the men of Group One to train again with Sergeant Rajit in the drill squad. The men who had not hacked off the legs of their *dungri* trousers wore Indian *dhotis* twisted around their loins. Many men also tied rags around their heads, knotted at four corners, to protect their newly shaven heads from the sun.

Rajit wore no shirt, his pot-belly hanging over the waistband of the trousers he had rolled to his knees. Looking short and roly-poly, he set the pace for the single-file line of men, surprising them with his energy, moving at a constant, staccato pace.

Leading the day's thirty-one-man squad down the rocky spine towards the cove, Rajit slowed as they reached Midshipman Bruce's carpenters working on the gallows. Rajit did not need to turn his head to know that the men behind him were gawking at the work being done.

"Eyes straight. You'll be up the gibbet soon enough."

"If I last out the day," called a voice.

Another man gulped, "I'll die before I get to the gibbet."

Rajit maintained a dog trot. "A man who's got wind enough to talk has wind enough to . . . *run!*" Quickening the pace, he bellowed, "Left! Left! Left! Left!"

Thirty-five minutes brought the men back around the rocky perimeter of Bull Island. They panted for air. Sweat covered their half-naked bodies. But Rajit still appeared fresh, his round, shaven head free from perspiration, looking as if he were starting the day's exercise.

At the crest of the hill, Rajit slowed the column as they approached Adam Horne standing by the sentry watch—Post One—commanding a view over the Arabian Sea to the east.

Horne fell into step with the squad to review Rajit's progress with the men, looking for stamina, comparing the performance of the prisoners to that of the ship's crew and the Marines, judging today's squad against the progress of the other three drill groups.

Running alongside George Tandimmer, he shouted, "Back straight, Tandimmer."

"Aye, aye, sir."

"Don't swing those arms, Tandimmer."

"Aye, aye, sir."

"Pull in that stomach, man."

"Aye, aye, sir."

"Tandimmer, you're a good sailor but you make a hell of a Marine."

The freckle-faced Sailing Master agreed loud and clear, *"Aye, aye, sir!"*

Horne left the column at the foot of the western slope as they began running towards the tumbledown buildings which had been the French prisons.

Rajit ordered, "Drop!"

The men fell to their stomachs on the ground.

"I didn't say lie down and go to sleep! I want you

to crawl! Crawl like the worms you are!"

Rajit moved along the string of gasping men, kicking them into a straight line, stepping on the buttocks of the men who arched too high off the ground.

"I said . . . *crawl!*"

The men bellied over the ground, approaching the area where small prisons had been chipped into the hard, yellow stone.

Rajit thundered, "Eyes right!"

The men looked to the right, seeing small, rectangular stone boxes topped with iron doors, one-man prisons in which a man lay on his back with the iron doors locked a few inches above his face, baking in the sun. The French had called the small prisons *"les fours"*—the ovens.

Rajit ordered, "Take a good look at those hot boxes. See what's waiting for you."

He walked alongside Mustafa the Turk.

"Do you see those rock beds, man?"

"Yes, sir." Mustafa kept his hips to the ground, face sideways, grimacing as he moved through the weeds.

Rajit passed down the line to the Japanese prisoner, Kiro, who was propelling himself with quick, strong movements of the elbows.

"Is there anything like these hot boxes where you come from?"

Kiro gritted his teeth as the hot sun beat down on his back. "No . . . sir."

"You're lucky. You'd still be inside one. Look at those shoulders—" Rajit lowered Kiro's neck with a stomp of the foot.

"And look at that butt!" Rajit's foot pressed Kiro's

groin to the ground. "I didn't tell you to kneel, damn it. I said 'crawl!' "

Horne had ordered the training to be concentrated on the fourteen prisoners from Bombay Castle. The men who proved to be the strongest were to bear the brunt of Rajit's discipline.

The next morning, work was completed on the gallows. Boards had been ripped from the steps and re-nailed across its legs and crossbeam, creating a wall atop the platform, a curtain of boards with a rope dangling from top to base.

Rajit led the day's new squad of twenty-nine men—Group Two—twice round the island, slowing them as they approached the gallows.

He turned and ran backwards, shouting to the men behind him, "Watch me close because I'm only going to show you bastards once."

Turning round again, he gathered speed and approached the gallows at a run, balancing his way up a protecting timber remaining from the dismantled steps. He leaped onto the platform, grabbed for the rope and began a hand-over-hand climb up the wall, knees straight, feet climbing the boards.

Reaching the top, he grasped the wall with one arm, dropped the rope and jumped for the mud pit which had been dug at the back of the gallows to break a man's fall. Loud hoots greeted him as he emerged from the base of the gallows, wiping mud from his face.

Good humouredly accepting the laughter, Rajit began barking the first man up the front of the gallows.

"Walk the wall, McFiddich. Hold onto the rope and walk that castle wall."

Kevin McFiddich grabbed the rope, moving his bare feet up the splintery boards.

"Drop the rope, McFiddich, and grab for the top."

McFiddish balanced himself at the top of the wall, tossed back the rope and held onto the wall.

"Bend your knees before you jump, McFiddich, or you're going to break your bloody legs."

McFiddich, knees bent, jumped for the mud pit.

Rajit hurried the next prisoner, Fred Babcock, up the gallows, yelling for him to walk the castle wall, toss back the rope, bend his knees before he jumped.

Rajit shouted the twenty-nine men through the gallows climb. He repeated the drill three times before running the men down to the cove, ordering them to dive into the clear blue water and wash their mud-covered bodies before jogging back to the settlement for their midday meal.

Fresh fish. Rice. Dates. Oranges. Tankards of cool beer drawn from kegs brought ashore and stored in the island's deep cellar. Simple but healthy, the fare was more appetizing than the usual midday meal of salt fish and dried biscuits aboard the *Eclipse*.

The men lined in front of a makeshift table set up beyond the barracks. After heaping their tin plates with food, they divided into small groups under rattan shelters dotting the hill which rose from the harbour.

Kevin McFiddich and Tom Gibbons sat side-by-side in a group of seven men under a sun shelter on the slope's western edge. McFiddich and Gibbons had become friends since Horne had locked them in bilboes.

Both men had finished their plates of food and listened quietly to the other five complaining about morning drill.

Ned Wren, a young yardsman with red hair and a blue rag tied like a cape over the sun blisters rising on his shoulders, cradled his right foot on his left thigh, picking splinters from his horny skin. "Why do sailors have to climb gallows and hurdle stone walls? It makes no damn sense to me."

Fernando Vega lay at the edge of the group, thinking about his wife, wondering if she had seen other men since he had been sent away to prison for murdering one of her admirers. Feeling cheated by life, his voice was thin with bitterness as he said, "Captain Horne wants to make Marines out of us."

Ned Wren kept digging at the sole of his foot. "Not me, jack. I sail for John Company but that don't make me no bloody Marine."

Martin Allen peeled an orange as he asked Wren, "What's Horne like? You sailed with him before."

"Ask Gibbons. He's been with Horne longer than me."

Gibbons sat feeling the smooth spots on both cheeks where his bushy muttonchop whiskers had grown until four days ago. "Don't ask me about Horne," he said glumly. "I don't know him. Not no more. He was always pokerfaced but a man who watched out for his crew. All that's changed now. You saw how he hit me. You saw how he beat me in the ribs. Humiliating me in front of my mates."

McFiddich listened to Gibbons complaining and,

hoping to encourage the big boatswain's ill-feelings, he patted him on his broad shoulder. "Look at it this way, Gibbons," he said consolingly. "It's good you found out what Horne's really like. Now we know what to watch out for."

Kevin McFiddich's body was lean and sinewy. His closely cut hair gave his face a skeletal look, making his eyes appear to be deeply set in their sockets. He had been press-ganged from the Lincolnshire Prison into His Britannic Majesty's Navy and had been gaoled three years later in Bombay Castle. He never talked about his crimes.

"I sailed three years aboard the *Land of Hope* so I know what I'm talking about." McFiddich's piercing dark eyes studied the six other men in the group. "Horne's ignoring all the rules. Doing what he damn well pleases."

Ned Wren straightened his right leg from his thigh. "I was seven years aboard the *Treaty*. I know other Marine captains don't run their ships like Horne. No officer makes his crew crawl through no bloody weeds. Look here at my belly. Look at these scratches . . ."

McFiddich raised his hand. "Why does Horne want to make Marines out of you? Like he says he's going to do with us new men? That's what's not clear to me."

He looked at the sunburnt faces around him. "I don't know about the rest of you but I don't want to be no Bombay Marine."

Wren glanced over his shoulder, confiding in a lower voice, "I don't even know if I want to be crew for Horne no more. That's how I'm thinking."

McFiddich's dark eyes glowed like two shining

chunks of coal in their sockets. "So let's get a plan."

He looked at Fred Babcock. "How about you, Babcock? Are you going to let Horne make you keep scrubbing deck whenever he wants to humiliate *you*?"

Babcock shrugged, pulling on one ear.

McFiddich glanced at the bare-knuckle fighter. "And what about you, Allen? You got family at home. Don't you want to go back to them?"

Martin Allen nodded slowly. "More than anything in the world."

McFiddich nodded at the small building which stood at the end of the wharf and served as Horne's Headquarters. "That's where our plan starts. Right down there."

The other six men looked at Headquarters. They saw Jingee approaching the front door with a covered tray in his hands.

McFiddich curled his upper lip with disgust. "Look at that poor bastard. See what Horne has him doing. Does Horne want to make Marines out of us like he says? Or is he going to train us to wait on him hand and foot?"

Martin Allen watched Jingee enter Headquarters. "I talked to that little Indian guy. His name's Jingee. He's not bad. He likes cooking and working for Horne."

McFiddich scoffed, "Then maybe this . . . Jingee's trying to be Horne's pet."

Vega interrupted. "Forget about the Indian, McFiddich. Tell us your plan."

McFiddich studied Vega's face, strong Latin features drawn tight with hatred and jealousy. "How do I know you're not going to run and tell Horne our plan? Try to be one of his pets yourself?"

Vega's chest swelled. "You insult me, McFiddich."

McFiddich smirked. "So what if I do, Spanish?"

"My name is not 'Spanish.' "

"To me it is."

"And to me you are . . . *caja* . . . shit!"

McFiddich rose to his knees.

Grabbing McFiddich by the elbow, Tom Gibbons whispered, "Kev, hold it. Fighting's not going to do nobody no good. We learned that."

McFiddich's deeply set eyes glared at Vega. "This greaser better watch it."

Vega's fists were clenched. "You've got to prove yourself worthy before we listen, McFiddich."

"I don't have to prove nothing to you, Spanish."

Babcock broke the tension with a laugh. "What about me? You said yourself, McFiddich, I'm not Horne's pet. Maybe you'll tell me your plan."

Wren chorused, "I want to hear too."

Martin Allen joined in. "You said something about me going home, McFiddich. I want to hear what you got to say."

McFiddich sank back onto the ground. He looked from Allen to Wren to Babcock. Glancing around the hillside for eavesdroppers, he turned to Vega and threatened, "If one word of what I'm going to say gets out, Spanish, I know exactly where to look for the rat."

He proceeded to explain his plan for escape, keeping his voice low as he told the six men what he wanted them to do.

11

Bite If You Can't Kick

The sixth day was over. Adam Horne sat contentedly on the bench outside Headquarters, boots crossed in front of him, facing the *Eclipse* riding high beyond the pier, a single lantern shining on the starboard gangway, a beacon for the next watch.

The challenge of settling Bull Island and establishing a training schedule had invigorated Horne. He felt alive, confident, enthusiastic about moulding a squadron of fit men to follow him into whatever waited at Fort St. George for the Bombay Marine. With the first week of physical training nearly complete, he knew that the rigid programme puzzled the men but, thankfully, no one had openly questioned their orders since arrival. He was pleased not to have had to make another ugly example of discipline as he had done aboard the *Eclipse*.

Living with day-to-day developments of accommodation and training, Horne was beginning to feel more satisfied that he could meet Commodore Watson's deadline. But the future—like the past—had little meaning to him these days. He was living and breathing the demands of Bull Island, and enjoying it.

As he thought about his own schedule, he felt hunger pangs and remembered that no food tray had appeared tonight on his desk in Headquarters. Either Jingee had forgotten to prepare his supper or the day's work had finally sapped the dubash's store of energy. Horne suspected that Jingee was asleep like the other one-hundred-and-eleven men not on duty tonight.

Rising from the bench, he decided to make the rounds of the sentry posts before looking for something to sate his hunger, a handful of dates, a few oranges, anything left over from the men's evening meal.

Stepping inside Headquarters, he struck a flint light and studied the guard list posted on the wall. He saw the names of the men standing watch at the three sentry posts and grabbed two clay pipes and a pouch of tobacco from the shelf. He tucked them into his shirt pocket and locked the door behind him.

The surf boomed beyond the rocks edging the island's eastern shore, the rollers crashing like cannon fire on the jagged shoreline, erupting into tiny pinpoints of spray and creaming into foamy tide.

Horne climbed the hill above the thundering surf, both hands tucked into his waistband, deciding that the time had come to alter the training schedule. Tomorrow morning he would tell Sergeant Rajit to slacken pace on the majority of men, to concentrate on the fit and able. That would leave three weeks to develop a small, tight squadron for the mission.

Three of the ship's seventeen Marines—Tyson Lovett, Randy Sweetwater, and Jim Davis—were proving to be in better condition than Horne had expected. He was also now able to count seven men from the ship's crew who had become hearty enough to be considered for a special Marine squadron. If Tom Gibbons gave him some sign that he was dependable, Horne could raise the number to eight.

Reaching the top of the hill, Horne counted over to himself the prisoners who might possibly be of use to him.

Mustafa the Turk was strong, well-disciplined, as skilful at firing muskets and fighting with knives as he was at swinging his garrotte. But Mustafa was a quiet man, always behaving so secretively. Did he have something to hide? If so, what was it? Was he a potential mutineer?

Kiro also puzzled Horne. The Japanese gunner backed away from all physical confrontation. Why? Was Kiro the kind of man who tightened in action? Or was he simply cowardly?

The Glaswegian prisoner, Brian Scott, was well-built, nimble, and not frightened to take chances. But Scott was always creating a disturbance. He accidentally knocked over poles, dropped a knife or flintlock with a loud clatter, coughed or sneezed at the wrong moment. Soldiers often had to be quiet but Scott could not stand still without making a noise.

The two prisoners who worried Horne the most were Babcock and McFiddich. Neither man had shown any signs of disobedience since arriving on Bull Island. Although Babcock never remembered to address an of-

ficer with respect and McFiddich's burning eyes
always seemed to be hiding a secret, so far both men
had obeyed Rajit's orders. They learned quickly. They
were proving to be strong and brave. Nevertheless,
something about them troubled Horne.

At the summit of the hill, he called out in the night
to identify himself to Tyson Lovett and the prisoner
whom Lovett had chosen for sentry partner, Martin Allen. Horne produced the pipes and tobacco for the men
as they set down the butts of their muskets on the stony
ground.

Tyson Lovett, a forty-two year-old Marine, broad-
chested, with straw-coloured hair and large glassy blue
eyes, helped himself to the tobacco as he reported,
"All's clear again tonight, sir."

Horne looked towards the southern horizon.

Martin Allen took the tobacco pouch from Lovett,
scooping a bowlful of rough brown shreds as he asked,
"You say, sir, that the French sail these waters?"

Horne detected a slight hesitation in the young bare-
knuckle fighter's voice. "The French have their southern base in Mauritius."

Allen puffed on the pipe's long stem, making the
bowl glow in the darkness. "What about the other islands out there, Captain? They have people living on
them?"

Allen's question might be innocent but Horne worried about the prisoners becoming too interested in the
surrounding islands. The Laccadives could be used as
an escape route to the mainland.

"Allen, your guess is as good as mine about what's
out there."

The young bare-knuckle fighter took another quick draw on the pipe.

Horne added, "Just follow orders, Allen, and you might get back to Stepney sooner than you think."

Allen's head jerked. "Stepney?"

"Isn't that home for you?"

"How do you know?"

The question had unnerved Allen. Why?

"I read your record at the Castle, Allen. I saw you have a wife at home." Horne did not divulge, however, that he had also read that Allen was illiterate, or that the Company Service officer had put down his suspicions that Allen applied himself so feverishly to exhibition fighting to compensate for the fact that he could not read or write.

Allen had tightened into a shell, his eyes lowered, his voice thinning as he admitted, "Yes, I have a missus. Her name's Ellen. We have a little one. He'll be four come April. I've never seen him."

Horne tried to be light-hearted. "I think I can safely say you won't be home for your son's next birthday. But you might well make it back next year."

Allen's eyes widened. "Sir, you think so?"

"I'm not making any promises. But I can do this much. Come and see me in Headquarters in the next couple of days. We'll see about sending a letter home to your wife."

"Sir, would you help me write it?"

Horne had learnt that seamen who openly admitted their illiteracy were more trustworthy than men who were ashamed of the fact.

"Come and see me, Allen, and I'll see your wife gets a letter from you."

Lingering a few more minutes with the two men before bidding them goodnight, Horne took the pipes and tobacco pouch for the guards on Post Two.

Hands gripped behind his back, head bent forward, he ambled down the western side of the plateau, wondering as he walked what it would be like to have a family waiting for you to come home. A son you've never seen. A wife.

The thought of being married, of having a family, reminded him of Isabel and his week-long contentment cracked with the image of her oval face, soft chestnut hair, eyes the colour of aquamarines. Would she have borne him children had she lived? A son? Daughters? Where would they have made their home? London? Or would she have taken the children to live with her father in Essex? Or would Horne's own father have given them the house in Mount Street in London?

Remembering how anxious Isabel had been to taste everything in life, Horne thought she would probably have wanted to come with him to India, to live in Bombay, build a little garden house with a view of Elephant Rock.

Slowing his pace with the bittersweet memory of Isabel, he realised that if she had lived, he would most likely not have come to India. His life would have been completely different. But having lost Isabel, he had replaced her with a continent. A strange country. A new life. Was it a fair substitute or was he hiding here from reality?

Unable now to stop his rush of memories and re-

flections, he wondered if a man who truly cared about
a foreign country should not be learning more about
it? Acquainting himself with the people and their
ways? Eating more of their food? Learning at least a
few words of their language and history?

Horne disapproved of colonial families who brought
English lives with them to India, lock, stock, and barrel. But had he not done worse? Was he not living in
a movable shell he had locked himself into years ago?
Wallowing in melancholy and self-pity?

Perhaps he was making himself a hermit as well.
Keeping himself too guarded from society when he
was ashore. Should he look for someone—something—
to replace Isabel? To be the new centre of his life apart
from work? But what about the idea he had entertained,
of never becoming attached to anybody, of protecting
himself from more disappointment? Was that cowardly? Unadventurous? Even puerile?

A sound disturbed him at the foot of the hill.

Horne stopped at the sound of the noise, studying two
roofless buildings in the moonlight, the tumbledown
stone structures which had once been the French prisons but now looked like jagged boulders in the darkness.

Again he heard the noise, a grunt like an animal.

Moving towards the larger of the two ruins, Horne
realised the sound had come from one of the shallow
prisons chipped into the ground, the stone prison dug
only a few yards away from him.

The prison's iron doors were closed. Horne moved
closer, seeing an iron pin holding them shut.

He heard the noise again. This time it sounded like a muffled call.

Bending over the rusty doors, he removed the pin and raised one door with a screech of metal. He saw the wrist of a man's bare arm chained to a metal ring. Hurriedly he opened the second door and recognized the man. Dropping to his knees, he pulled the rag from Jingee's mouth and began freeing his arms from the iron rings.

Jingee remained silent as Horne released him, scrambling from the prison as Horne stood up.

"Jingee, who did this to you?"

Jingee did not answer. He stood with his eyes to the ground.

"Jingee, why aren't you talking?"

Jingee shook his head.

"Are you refusing to tell me who locked you in there?"

Jingee began to speak but stopped.

"Jingee, I can't make you talk. But I know you're an intelligent man so I can ask you to *think* about what happened to you. I want you to think how this could affect the other men and I want you to come and see me tomorrow morning."

Horne escorted Jingee to his barracks in silence. He waved him past the guard and turned to the cove.

Forgetting about hunger, he felt a foul mood overtaking him, discontentment with Jingee and agitation with all the crew.

Horne had to be so many things to his men. Teacher. Warden. Sleuth. Disciplinarian. The responsibility could sometimes feel unbearable, especially at these times when he wanted nothing more than to have a simple existence, to be a husband and father, to have a chance of that life which had been destroyed on the night when Isabel had been shot.

Unbuckling his belt and pulling off his shirt, Horne began dropping his clothes as he moved towards the end of the pier. The only panacea for despair was to keep in motion, to exhaust the body until the mind was dull.

His naked body sliced the ruffled water in a neat, silent dive.

Jingee lay awake in his hammock in the darkness of the barracks. He held both hands clasped behind his neck, thinking about the three men who had locked him in the shallow stone prison earlier tonight when he had been on his way to Headquarters with Horne's supper. The men were English and had called Jingee the "Captain's pet." It was not the first time that Jingee had been called such a name.

From childhood, Jingee had been smaller than other boys. His parents had taught him that he must acquire abilities which taller, stronger boys did not possess. They had tutored him to read, to write, to cook and sew, to do menial tasks which men—even women—considered unworthy for people in their high station of society, the *Vaisya* caste.

Unlike many Tamils, Jingee's parents had interpreted the coming of the *feringhi*—foreigners—to India as the end of life as their ancestors had known it. The Muslim Mughul had begun changing India three hundred years ago. Dutch and Portuguese traders had

come next, bringing their ships and strange plants—
potatoes and corn. Now it was the English.

Apart from learning how to make himself indispen-
sible to powerful conquerors with his talents and skills,
Jingee had also learnt how to protect himself.

His father had taught him to fight, beginning by giving the basic advice that if you are too small to strike
your adversary, then kick him, and if you can't kick,
then bite him—to do anything to protect yourself and
your honour.

Thinking about the men who had locked him in the
shallow prison tonight, Jingee lay in the hammock and
began plotting his revenge against their leader and in-
stigator, Kevin McFiddich. He was sorry that his revenge would anger Horne. Horne was a good man, a
rare *feringhi* who, despite his strength, was a feeling,
sensitive man. Jingee greatly respected him. But Jingee
also respected himself, and he decided to fight Mc-
Fiddich with the same weapon which he had used to
kill the English factor in Hyderabad. Jingee knew, too,
where he would get the knives.

12

Burn in Hell

Adam Horne did not know how long he had been swimming when he pulled himself onto the pier, but his muscles ached and his brain was numb from the physical exertion. Grabbing his clothes from the wharf, he dried himself with his shirt as he padded in darkness towards Headquarters.

He collapsed onto the cot and the next thing he knew somebody was pounding on the door, shouting, "Captain Horne! Wake up, Captain Horne! There's trouble!"

Horne leaped out of the cot. He looked through the small window above the cot and saw dawn bleaching the sky.

Pulling on his breeches as he moved towards the door, he lifted the latch and found Midshipman Bruce standing outside on the doorstep.

The round-cheeked Midshipman snapped a salute, blurting, "Sir, there's a fight by the Barracks!"

Horne's mind cleared. "Where's Sergeant Rajit?"

"Aboard the *Eclipse*, sir. I sent the Dutchman, Groot, to fetch him, sir."

Horne grabbed for his boots. "Who's fighting?"

"McFiddich and your man, sir."

Horne stood like a stork in the middle of the room, one boot in mid-air. "*My* man?"

"The prisoner called Jingee, sir. The man who cooks and washes for you."

Horne drove his foot into the boot with a slam.

Bruce held both arms stiff at his side. "It appears, sir, that your man started the fight."

Horne buckled his belt, thinking that if Jingee had instigated a fight with McFiddich it meant that it was McFiddich who had locked him in the prison last night. Jingee was seeking revenge. Horne cursed himself for not suspecting what Jingee would do. It was the natural action for a man who put so much store in honour and self-respect, for someone who had been imprisoned for murdering a foreigner who had violated Hindu caste laws.

"Are you armed, Bruce?"

"Yes, sir. A brace of pistols."

"Good. What barracks is it?"

"Barracks One, sir."

"Who's on guard there this morning?"

"Wheeler, sir. He has that big African as his partner. Both men are armed with muskets, sir, but they're waiting for your orders to fire."

"Let's go."

Horne led Bruce out of the door.

• • •

The two men crossed the harbour yard at a quick pace, approaching a crowd encircling the front of the stone-and-mortar shed known as Barracks One.

The men parted for Horne to pass through the circle, all except for Tom Gibbons who stood in Horne's path. "Your man started it, Captain Horne."

Horne pushed Gibbons aside and continued through the crowd, halting when he saw McFiddich and Jingee, both crouching forward and armed with knives.

The circle closed round Horne as he faced the fighters and shouts rose for the favorite.

"Watch out for him, Kev."

"Take him slow, McFiddich."

"Clip his other wing, McFiddich. Go for him. Go for him."

McFiddich played his knife with back flips of the wrist, stepping on one foot, then the other, revolving clockwise around Jingee.

Jingee wore his usual white turban and *dhoti*. His bare feet danced in constant movement as he stabbed his blade at McFiddich, poking the knife back and forth in the air until—in a flash—he lunged for his opponent.

McFiddich dodged. But Jingee's knife nicked his shoulder cap and a line of scarlet trickled down McFiddich's bicep.

Horne reached back so that Midshipman Bruce could hand him the pistols. Taking the primed flint-locks, he stepped forward and shouted, "Enough!"

Jingee faltered.

McFiddich seized his opportunity and stabbed for Jingee.

Jingee smiled. He had anticipated McFiddich's movement. He stepped to his left and McFiddich fell face down on the ground.

Pouncing onto McFiddich's back like a cheetah, Jingee locked both legs around the other man's shoulders and clenched a forearm around his neck, positioning the knife to his throat.

Horne kicked the knife from Jingee's hand and, raising both pistols, pointed a barrel at each man. "Move and I'll blow your brains out."

McFiddich lay gasping on his stomach, loosening the hold on his knife. But Jingee remained where he was, both legs locked over McFiddich's shoulders.

Horne pressed the barrel against Jingee's temple. "I said stop."

Jingee remained firmly on McFiddich's back.

Horne clicked the pistol's hammer.

Dropping his arm, Jingee slumped to the ground.

Horne beckoned to one of the Marines, Wheeler. "Seize the weapons."

Stepping back while the Marine retrieved the two knives, he looked from Jingee to McFiddich. "Who got the knives?"

Jingee's voice was quiet, respectful. "Me, Captain sahib. From the kitchen."

"Did McFiddich lock you in the prison last night, Jingee?"

McFiddich raised from the ground. "Yes. But so what? That's where pets belong, isn't it? Locked in cages?"

Horne swung the flintlock against the side of McFiddich's head.

McFiddich's body slumped to the ground and, standing over it, Horne ordered, "Wheeler, escort this man to the old prison grounds. Lock him in one of the small prisons. Midshipman Bruce will accompany you with padlock and chains."

"Yes, sir."

Horne raised his voice. "Has Sergeant Rajit returned to shore yet?"

Rajit's voice boomed behind him. "Here, suh!"

Horne kept his eyes on Jingee as he ordered, "Sergeant, I want you to take this other man aboard the *Eclipse*. I want him locked in bilboes. If he gives you any trouble, tie his hands behind his back, shoot him in both legs, and throw him overboard."

"Yes, suh!"

In the circle of men behind Horne, Fred Babcock looked from Tom Gibbons to Martin Allen to Fernando Vega, at all eleven men so far recruited for the escape plot. How did McFiddich's imprisonment affect the mutiny? Babcock suspected that the time had come for him to start making his own plans.

Kevin McFiddich's wrists and ankles were bound tightly to the iron rings embedded into the floor of the stone prison. He lay spreadeagled on his back under the rusty iron doors and, as the late morning sun fired the metal above his face, he kept turning his head from left to right, trying to avoid the blistering heat.

Salty rivulets of sweat flooded his eyes. The heat dried his lips. Thickened his tongue. Parched his throat. He called for the guards to give him water but nobody replied.

He kept turning his head from side to side. He wiggled his fingers in the chains. He took deep gulps of air. He did everything he could to quiet his heartbeat, hoping to calm the panic caused by the iron doors locked shut a few inches above his eyes.

Periodically, he heard the sound of the drill squad as they rounded the island. When they stopped passing his prison, McFiddich guessed that it must be midday, and that the men had gone to eat under the sun shelters on the hillside.

To keep his mind off hunger and thirst, he studied a small shaft of light piercing the stonework to the right of his head. He saw an ant crawling along the stones and moving towards the iron doors above him.

The ant was joined by a second ant, larger and red and crawling faster than the first ant.

A third ant joined them, and another, and another . . .

McFiddich's body was covered with ants. There were ants on his arms, ants crawling across his neck, between his shoulder blades, through his crotch, into his ears, up his nostrils . . .

Telling himself he was only imagining that he was lying on an anthill, he tried to forget about the present and to concentrate on the past, to remember life as it had been before he had been imprisoned in Bombay Castle.

A woman's voice hissed in his ear.

May you burn forever in hell!

Kevin McFiddich had been imprisoned for rape. He had accosted a scrivener's wife in a back alley of Bombay. Her name was Jane Morgan and McFiddich had made the mistake of going into the bazaar, so giving

Jane Morgan the opportunity to identify him to patrol guards.

Flaxen-haired and fair-skinned, Jane Morgan had attended McFiddich's hearing in Bombay Castle. She had sat silently in her chair throughout the trial. But when the time came for the sentence to be read, she sprang from the chair, pointing her finger at McFiddich and cursing, "May you and every man like you burn forever in hell!"

Burn in hell.

Had Jane Morgan put a curse on him? Was it coming to pass? Had she willed him into this prison?

But why had he not suffered from other curses in the past? What about the women he had taken in England? The cobbler's daughter? The tiny-boned dressmaker? The housemaid with raven locks who had bitten him so hard when he had held his hand over her mouth? Why had none of his other victims cursed him like Jane Morgan?

A sudden tap, tap, tap on the iron doors brought McFiddich's thoughts back to the present and he thought that someone had finally come to free him.

The tapping sound continued. McFiddich's heart sank as he realised that the noise was not someone tapping a signal to him: it was the pounding of heavy raindrops on the iron doors.

The sound of rain grew louder, falling faster on the doors, the shower quickly becoming a deluge, and the vent which had admitted light to McFiddich's shallow prison now channelled torrents of water into the rock box.

As the rain fell harder, water began to rise around

McFiddich's body, flooding him with dirt and floating insects and more water. McFiddich began to dig with his fingernails, to claw at the rocks in his shackles. The manacles burned the skin on his wrists. The irons rubbed against his ankles. But he tried to claw, to kick, to gouge some kind of niche or hole for the water to escape from this quickly-filling reservoir.

A voice outside the prison stopped him. Who was it? He listened.

The voice called, "Kev?"

"Who is it?"

"Kev, it's Tom here. Tom Gibbons. Don't talk, Kev. Just listen . . ."

"Gibbons, get me out of here! Damn it to hell, Gibbons, I'm drowning in here!"

"The rain's stopped, Kev. You'll be okay. There's a change of guard coming on duty. Just try to hold on till tonight."

"You going to help me, Gibbons?"

"We're going to help you. We got more men. One's the guard coming on duty with Vega."

"Promise me! Promise me you're going to help me!"

"I promise you, McFiddich. I promise."

McFiddich heard the sound of footsteps crunching away from him and he relaxed, smiling at the thought that he would soon be free to sail for Oman.

Tom Gibbons walked slowly away from McFiddich's prison, filled with sudden doubts about the man who had become his new friend.

Gibbons tried to imagine how Adam Horne would act if he were locked in a prison like McFiddich.

Would Horne beg to be let out? Would Horne panic? Call to be rescued?

Gibbons suspected that if Horne suffered it would be in silence.

Only a few weeks ago it had been an honour for Gibbons to serve under Horne. The mission to the North Arabian Sea had been a high point of his life. He had gone with Horne into the Maratha camp in the hills above the Gulf of Maniy. He had fought with a dirk and a branch from a tree. Horne had praised him for his courage and Gibbons had never felt prouder.

But ten days ago Gibbons's world had collapsed. He had fought with Kevin McFiddich aboard the *Eclipse* and Horne had humiliated him in front of the crew. Gibbons could not forgive the Captain for doing such a thing to him. Nevertheless, he was still secretly ashamed that he had to throw in his lot with a man as gutless as McFiddich.

Sergeant Rajit saw that the day was progressing from bad to worse.

Two men collapsed from heat stroke during morning drill. Before midday, Tyson Lovett spotted the sails of an unidentifiable brig against the southern horizon as Rajit passed the Sentry Post with the drill squad. By the time that Horne had rushed from Headquarters with his spyglass, the mysterious ship had disappeared. Later, the deluge had collapsed the roof on Barracks Two and, after the midday meal, Rajit sprained his ankle in the gallows jump.

Frustrated, he sat on the edge of a cot in Flannery's

makeshift infirmary and insisted that he could walk, that the injury was not serious.

Flannery knelt in front of him on the dirt floor, examining the ankle. "Just take a swig of that bottle I gave you, bucko, and let me do the deciding about what's serious or not."

The pain throbbed up Rajit's leg but he was determined not to complain. Being a teetotaller, and knowing that Flannery was a tippler, he was also determined not to drink from the small brown bottle which Flannery had given him.

"Take a drink of that medicine," the Irishman urged, "or you'll never get out of here."

Rajit bit back a scream as the pain shot through his leg, and, recognizing the Sergeant's stubbornness, Flannery twisted the ankle more ruthlessly.

Rajit's scream filled the room.

"Are you ready to listen to me, bucko?"

Rajit gulped at the bottle.

"Aye, that's a good lad."

Rajit's mouth felt sticky, coated with a sweet-tasting film. Looking at the bottle he had half-emptied, he asked, "What is this?"

Flannery ignored the question. "You've got to stay off your feet for two, maybe three weeks. Read some of those fine books of yours."

"I can't stay off my feet for two weeks. Horne can't drill those men without . . ."

Rajit stopped. He felt dizzy. His head was spinning. "What kind of medicine was that you . . . gave me?"

Flannery moved across the room to make a salt bath. "Laudanum."

"Laudan . . ." Again, Rajit faltered, shaking his head. He felt drowsy.

Returning to the bed with a basin, Flannery found his patient slumped across the mattress. He smiled at the pot-bellied Asian. There was a way to handle men who wouldn't listen to him.

Setting down the salt bath on the floor, he pulled his brandy flask from his pocket. Feeling the liquor burn his throat, he thought how much closer he was to subduing—once and for all—the man who had killed his dearly beloved brother thirty-one years ago. Laudanum would be child's play compared to the weapon he would use in his vendetta. Flannery's lips lifted in a thin smile.

13

The Chosen Few

Adam Horne awoke on the seventh morning in Headquarters with one thought foremost in his mind: he was wrong to weigh himself down with the problems that had developed on Bull Island when the goal of his mission was not here but at Fort St. George.

As he shaved and dressed, he realised that he would utilize his time better by relegating all administrative duties—including discipline—to his officers and concentrating his own efforts on choosing the final candidates for the squadron.

Thinking about his officers, Horne remembered how Tim Flannery had reported last night that Sergeant Rajit's ankle would take ten days to two weeks to mend. Horne wanted Rajit with him at Fort St. George and, as departure was only three weeks away, he faced the fact that Rajit would have to stay off his feet and not help him in preparing the team.

Glancing out of the window as he dried himself, he

looked across the harbour yard at the men pouring
from the two barracks. Why not begin separating the
wheat from the chaff this morning at breakfast? By the
end of the day's drill, he could make the next elimi-
nations.

Of the one-hundred-and-twenty men on Bull Island,
Horne suspected there would be little more than a
dozen or so potential candidates for the mission. Why
not start discovering today exactly how many fit and
truly able men he had?

Leaving Headquarters, he crossed the yard at a smart
pace, feeling enthusiasm for the work building inside
him. It was the same glow of excitement he had felt
before the fight between Jingee and McFiddich. Perhaps he was losing himself in duty, but the spark of
renewed energy made every problem seem surmount-
able again.

"Groot, climb that wall! There's a hound snapping at
your arse . . . Can't bloody Turks jump higher than a
foot off the ground, Mustafa? . . . You're a good shot
with a musket, Bapu, but you throw that grappling iron
like a girl."

Adam Horne heard himself mimicking Rajit's staccato commands as he pushed the sixteen men he had
selected at breakfast through the drill courses dotted
around Bull Island. As the morning sun crested in the
sky, he led the single file of men over stone hurdles,
snaked them on their bellies across stony ground and
improvised bridges, barked them up greased poles
planted in sand.

"Babcock, when I say run, you ask 'how far, *sir*?'

. . . Put more weight into that first, Kiro. You're not going to kill a man with your knuckles. Not the way you hit . . . Sweetwater, you tackle that sandbag like an old maiden aunt."

Three of Horne's training team came from the *Eclipse's* Marine unit, Tyson Lovett, Cable Wendell and Randy Sweetwater. Brett Dunbar and Geoff Hands belonged to the ship's crew. The other eleven men were prisoners from Bombay Castle: Allen, Bapu, Babcock, Kiro, Groot, Jud, Mustafa, Poiret, Quinte, Scott and Vega.

Horne broke drill for the midday meal earlier than Rajit's usual hour, but instead of allowing the team time to rest after eating, he ordered them back up on their feet and began them running in the blazing sun. Groaning, the men trudged from the island's main settlement towards the southern plateau, dragging their feet up the slope, a few vomiting as they mounted the hill.

Horne pushed them, and when Randy Sweetwater was unable to rise from the ground, he left him on his knees retching, the first man to be eliminated from the final contenders for the mission.

As the sun began sinking towards the western horizon, Horne detailed the remaining fifteen men to dig new latrines, split firewood, mend fishnets and join guard duty. He moved from post to post, observing which men still had some energy after a gruelling day's exercises, which men complained about long hours, which men pushed themselves to obey orders.

The time came for supper, but Horne postponed his own meal. He remained in Headquarters to inform two more men that he was eliminating them from the squadron.

Brian Scott, brawny and loyal, did not understand silence. Horne hated to lose a rugged man like Scott but one badly timed cough, one clank of the musket could betray a unit's location and endanger the entire mission.

The next man to be dismissed was Kiro. The Japanese prisoner stood barefooted in front of Horne's desk, a *dhoti* tied around his sinewy body and a red bandana twisted around his forehead.

Horne paced the floor behind Kiro. "You're strong. Quick. You have stamina. You're good at everything except a hand-to-hand fight."

Silently, Kiro stood facing Horne's desk.

"For some reason, Kiro, you freeze at the moment of attack. Why?"

Kiro's voice was soft and respectful, touched with his musical Eastern accent. "My master taught me to show caution, Captain Horne."

Horne looked over his shoulder at Kiro. "Master?"

"Master of the Open Hand, sir."

Intrigued, Horne asked, "Your teacher of *Karate*?"

"Yes, sir."

Horne had forgotten about Kiro's knowledge of *Karate*; he had killed a man in Bombay Castle with one deft chop of the hand, and he might well worry about accidentally injuring someone.

The germ of an idea sprouting in his brain, Horne resumed his pacing of the room. "I learned from a man I respect very much, Kiro, that Greeks travelled to Japan hundreds of years ago, that they taught their art of openhand combat—*Pankration*—to the Japanese in exchange for the secret of silk-making."

Kiro remained facing the desk. "I have not heard that story, sir."

"If you turn round, Kiro, I'll show you the similarities I learned between Japanese *Karate* and Greek *Pankration*."

Horne raised both hands, holding both elbows downwards, resting his weight on his back foot as Elihu Cornhill had taught him.

Kiro turned and immediately recognized Horne's stance as a Japanese *kata*. Raising his own hands, Kiro rested his weight on his back leg, raising one heel of the other foot off the floor, toes pointed upwards.

Horne sliced one hand at Kiro.

Kiro blocked the chop, spinning, striking at Horne with his bare foot.

Horne stepped away from Kiro's kick, swinging his left hand for the next move. The two men continued in silent combat, one deft slice or kick following another, each block, each kick being potentially lethal had it struck its mark.

Satisfied, Horne stepped back from Kiro and dropped his arms.

"Kiro, why didn't you tell me you were worried about injuring somebody with your hands during training?"

Kiro's finely chiselled face remained placid but his dark eyes twinkled. "The Japanese also have the art of *Haiku*, Captain Horne. I do not know if we learned it from the Greeks but one poem says, 'Water changes to steel but leaves fall softly when the bird flies.' "

Horne returned to his desk. "Kiro, will you agree to keep training with the team?"

Both arms by his side, palms inwards, Kiro bowed to Horne.

The garish purple Indian sunset was darkening to an indigo night as Horne climbed into the jolly-boat to row out to the *Eclipse* for an overdue meeting with George Tandimmer. Since morning, he had enjoyed boundless energy. His list of chores seemed endless but he felt he could accomplish everything as long as he kept driving himself. In the rapidly spreading night, he was pushing the snubnosed boat from the pier when he heard Midshipman Bruce running towards him, calling, "Captain Horne! Captain Horne! A message from Sergeant Rajit, Captain Horne!" Horne leaned from the boat, grabbed the folded paper from Bruce's outstretched hand. Tucking it into his waistband, he hurried to stop one oar from slipping in its rowlock.

Tandimmer waited for Horne at the port entry of the *Eclipse*, pleased to be free from shore drills and honoured that Horne had invited him for a tankard of beer in the Captain's cabin.

The two men sat on opposite sides of the desk, in the breeze from the stern window. While enjoying Tandimmer's company, Horne also hoped to glean information from him about Madras.

Not wanting to arouse Tandimmer's suspicions about the *Eclipse's* destination after Bull Island, Horne manoeuvred the conversation towards the subject of native craft, eventually asking, "What's the name of those boats that carry passengers ashore at Madras?"

Tandimmer licked foam from his upper lips. *"Masulah."*

"What are they? Dug-out logs?"

"A *masulah*, sir, is a plank boat sewn together with coconut twine."

Horne was certain of Tandimmer's loyalty but Commodore Watson had given him strict orders not to tell anyone the few available details about the Governors' mission for the Bombay Marine.

He risked another question. "What shape are these boats?"

"Flat bottomed with tall sides inclining like—"

Tandimmer set his tankard on the corner of Horne's desk and slanted both hands inwards, "—like this."

Horne took another sip of his beer. "Odd shape for a shore boat."

Tandimmer explained. "There's no harbour at Madras, sir. Also, the surf's rough there and comes in three stages. When the first wave crashes ashore, the second is a hundred yards or so out, and the third wave is the same distance away again. All three race to shore in great, galloping speeds."

"And these *masulah* boats can withstand such a surf?"

"Oh, they leak and capsize every now and then, you can be certain of that. They're also known to dunk their passengers in the drink. That's why they're usually escorted by catamarans, to fish out the passengers. The *masulah* oarsmen wear tall, hollow hats to carry important papers back and forth between ship and shore."

Satisfied with these few details, Horne turned the conversation to the subject of catamarans, then to another unique Indian boat, a *gurab*, which the Bombay Marine had developed into a ship known to the English as a "grab."

Finally bidding Tandimmer good night, Horne saw him to the cabin door.

The Sailing Master hesitated in the companionway. "Sir, if you want to know more about the surf off Madras, you should ask Jingee. I talked with him on shore for several nights after supper and he told me his family have a fishing fleet near Cuddalore."

Horne knew that Jingee's family came from the Coromandel Coast, that they were rich merchants and members of the *Vaisya* Caste. He had not asked the Indian about Madras because a decision still had to be made about his punishment for fighting McFiddich.

He remembered another fact about Jingee. "Did he ever learn how to pronounce your name?"

Tandimmer's freckled face broke into a grin. "Tin hammer."

Horne extended his hand. "Good night."

"Good night, sir."

Horne closed the door, displeased that Tandimmer had reminded him about Jingee. He liked Jingee. Apart from being a devoted worker, the little man was good company. But he had done wrong in fighting with McFiddich and a decision had to be made soon about his punishment.

The sky glittered with small pinpoints of stars as Horne climbed the ladder to the quarterdeck and found Lieutenant Pilkington on watch.

Pilkington saluted Horne and returned to studying

the full phosphorescent moon swept by clouds. "A brisk westerly tonight, sir."

Horne nodded, wishing they could weigh anchor tonight for Madras and embark on whatever mission awaited them there. He was making headway on Bull Island but he was becoming impatient for real action, or at least to learn the exact orders for the Marines. His last assignment had been so clear cut, so concise in its instructions to stop Singee Ranjee attacking Company trade routes. He had known exactly how to prepare his men and ship, how to make the most of advantages and shortcomings.

"Sir, we were lucky today, weren't we?"

"Lucky, Lieutenant?"

"Not to have had another big downpour."

"Hmmm."

"I'll tell you now, sir, I wouldn't like to have been McFiddich in that hot box."

Horne did not want to talk about Kevin McFiddich any more than he had wanted to discuss Jingee, but as usual, Pilkington was eager to talk.

"Sir, do you imagine that if McFiddich were left long enough inside that hot box he would cook? Roast like a joint of beef?"

"Lieutenant, may we abandon the subject of Mc-Fiddich?"

"Yes, sir. Sorry, sir." Pilkington moved fore, leaving Horne by the taffrail.

Alone, Horne began pacing the quarterdeck, his thoughts moving from Jingee and McFiddich to his hesitation about deciding their punishment and so to the responsibility of a leader. Standing beneath the starry Indian sky, he clasped both hands behind his back and remembered how he had begun to understand the true challenges of leadership on the last assignment. He recalled his early years of military training with Elihu Cornhill, the squarely-built old soldier who had first tutored him in the art of leading others.

"A leader must remember two things, Horne. Never be without a command for your men, even if it's no more than 'show courage' . . . 'take cover' . . . 'prepare for action' . . .

"Secondly, Horne, always be prepared to get in and fight alongside your men. That doesn't mean relaxing discipline or becoming overly familiar. A leader must keep his men's respect while at the same time setting the example for them, showing them how to fight like a dog."

Elihu Cornhill had been fifty-seven years old when Horne had studied with him in Wiltshire, a veteran of the War of the Austrian Succession but a soldier who preferred to remember his years fighting North American Indians in Quebec.

Cornhill had taught his young pupils to cover their bodies with chimney soot and crawl through inky-black English nights. To cake their arms and legs with lead paint in winter and dash from poplar to poplar in a January snowfall, camouflaged against a winterscape of whiteness.

Food was as important in survival training as avoiding detection by the enemy. Cornhill had taught his students how to bite open a squirrel's neck, how to skin the fur from the rodent's warm body and devour its flesh raw. He had also taught his young men how a soldier could survive in prison by eating the callouses from his feet and hands.

The young men whom Elihu Cornhill selected to train came from all parts of Britain, from every walk of life—country bumpkins, city rakes, heirs to vast fortunes, destitute lads without even a pair of shoes to their name.

Were Cornhill's teachings eccentric, perhaps even dangerous? Were his students no more than an odd selection of boys playing exotic games of tin soldiers on a tumbledown Wiltshire estate?

Perhaps so. But whatever their background, Cornhill selected students who had had some brush with crime.

Grab a criminal early enough in life, Horne, and you might find a soldier.

Standing aboard the *Eclipse* off the rocky shore of Bull Island, Horne wondered if his idea to make Bombay Marines out of prisoners should really be attributed to Elihu Cornhill. Had the suggestion to recruit men from the dungeons of Bombay Castle stemmed from Cornhill's philosophy of giving a young man a chance to prove his worthiness on the battlefield, to serve King and Country rather than to murder, rob, and vandalise?

A splash in the water broke his reverie.

Standing motionless on the quarterdeck, he scanned the ruffled water between the *Eclipse* and the shoreline.

He spotted a swimmer approaching the frigate with strong, clean strokes.

A voice hailed from the water. "Ahoy! Permission to come aboard!"

Lieutenant Pilkington moved alongside Horne on the

quarterdeck, his hand resting on the hilt of his sabre.

Horne raised his hand. "I'll deal with this, Lieutenant."

Descending the ladder, Horne crossed to the port entry and cupped both hands to his mouth. "Identify yourself."

The swimmer's head bobbed below the bulwark, a round spot in the spreading glow from the port lantern.

"Babcock!"

Horne threw a rope.

Babcock's bare feet scrambled up the hull, his breath steady despite the climb and the long swim.

Standing in front of Horne, he dripped water onto the deck. "McFiddich's out."

"Out?"

"Of prison. Somebody set him loose."

Horne's dark eyes narrowed. "How do you know this, Babcock?"

"Mercer had me listed for guard duty with Rajit and—"

Horne sharply corrected, "You call him *Midshipman* Mercer, Babcock. And *Sergeant* Rajit."

"*Midshipman* Mercer had me listed for guard duty with *Sergeant* Rajit . . . sir. But I remembered that Rajit—*Sergeant* Rajit—twisted his ankle yesterday. So I goes to the Infirmary to see if there was some change of command. Rajit—*Sergeant* Rajit—he sent me to check with the old Marine, Witherspoon, who was standing guard duty tonight with Vega over McFiddich's hot box. That's when I saw it."

"Saw, Babcock?"

"McFiddich gone, Witherspoon too. And Vega dead."

"Vega . . . *dead*?"

Babcock sliced one finger across his throat.

Fernando Vega had trained all day with Horne. The Spanish prisoner was moody but had shown more energy than any other man on the team. Now he was dead. Horne was less one more man for Fort St. George.

Babcock continued. "I reported back to Rajit. That was when he—*Sergeant* Rajit, sir—told me to come out to you."

"Why didn't you row?"

"Rajit told me to draw as little attention to myself as possible."

The advice was sound. Horne wondered, however, if it had indeed come from Rajit. He remembered that Babcock had been part of the plot in Bombay Castle to get the cell keys. He also remembered seeing Babcock eating his midday meals with McFiddich.

Unable to tell from the big American Colonial's manner whether he was lying, Horne pressed, "What's happened to Vega's musket?"

"Gone."

"McFiddich's armed."

"Witherspoon too."

Horne waited a few seconds trying to evaluate Babcock's report. He had to admit that his manner was not altogether displeasing. Babcock was either a friendly man or a truly accomplished actor.

"Babcock, why do I think I can't believe you?"

Grinning, Babcock pulled on his ear. "I didn't think

you'd believe me, Captain, so I asked Rajit what I could tell you for proof."

"And?"

"He said he'd sent you a note earlier tonight."

Horne remembered the note which Midshipman Mercer had brought as he was leaving the pier in the jolly-boat. He took it from his waistband, unfolded it, and read the one word which Rajit had written on it.

"TROUBLE."

Horne made his decision. "I'm going back ashore with you, Babcock. We'll go the same way you came out. Swim."

14

The Mystery Ship

Horne and Babcock crawled from the surf a short distance along the shore from Headquarters. Still uncertain about Babcock's loyalties, Horne sent him to check on the sentry at the far side of the island. He remained crouched alongside the boulders until he saw Babcock disappear up the western slope. He made his own way in the opposite direction.

Tonight's guard at Headquarters were the two Marines, Cabel Williams and Jim Hobbs; Horne paused a few yards from the small house until he saw them turn towards the pier, then, dashing towards the building, he pressed himself against the plank door, reached sideways, turned the iron ring, and slipped across the threshold.

Accustoming his eyes to the faint light pouring through the small window above the cot, he heard snores come from a body heaped on the mattress—Midshipman Mercer.

Calvin Mercer jumped at the clamp of Horne's hand on his mouth.

Ready to defend himself if the young Midshipman struggled in his half-awake state, Horne whispered, "It's me . . . Captain Horne."

Mercer raised himself on his elbows, his dark eyes wide with surprise.

Horne kept his hand clamped over Mercer's mouth. "McFiddich's escaped."

Mercer's eyes shot above him to the window.

"He's got recruits."

Mercer sat higher on the cot.

"We can't trust more than a handful of men."

Mercer nodded.

"I want you to get dressed. Slip out of the window. Go down to Barracks One. You'll find Midshipman Bruce there on guard with Bapu."

Horne released his grip from Mercer's mouth. "One man's already been killed."

"Mutiny, sir?"

"It could be. So after alerting Midshipman Bruce, go to the Infirmary and wake Sergeant Rajit. Help him walk back here. Rajit can keep watch on the arsenal while you take command of Pier Guard."

"Yes, sir."

"Now get dressed."

Horne moved to his desk and removed a brace of pistols from the top drawer. He stuck them into the waistband of his soaked breeches and moved back to the bed while Mercer was pulling on his boots.

Standing by the window, Horne watched Williams and Hobbs pass in their patrol. He waited until they had turned the corner, then leaped onto the cot, pushed out the window frame and hopped onto the sill. Holding the framed glass, he jumped outside to the ground. Mercer followed him over the sill and disappeared into the night; then Horne replaced the pane.

Crouching in the darkness, Horne listened to Williams and Hobbs talking around the corner about the advantages of owning farmland as opposed to a public house.

When he finally moved from the shadows he kept low to the ground, dashing in short sprints across the barren space between Headquarters and the western slope of the island which rose jagged in the moonlight.

Horne made faster time moving on higher ground where he was protected by the silhouette of the cliffs and by the sound of the sea crashing against them. Pausing at the crest, he espied the dark shapes of two men ahead of him on the plateau: one man was kneeling in front of another who appeared to be propped against the trunk of a stunted tree.

"Horne?"

Horne froze at the call of his name.

The voice belonged to Babcock. "They got Allen, Horne."

If Babcock was a spy for McFiddich, he was a good one. Horne was impressed that the American had not only heard him climbing the slope but had identified him without turning his head.

Moving across the plateau, he fell to his knees next to Babcock; Martin Allen was propped against the trunk, blood soaking his shirt. Horne recalled fleetingly that Allen had also been among the prisoners training in today's drill team. Damn it! Did this mean he was one more man short for the squad?

Babcock tucked a folded shirt behind Allen's head. "Sweetwater was on duty here with Allen tonight."

"Sweetwater's joined McFiddich?" Horne remembered how Randy Sweetwater had collapsed in the sun after lunch. He wondered if the Marine had joined the mutineers out of revenge for being eliminated from the squad.

Allen's breath came in short spurts. "McFiddich stabbed me when I said . . . I said I wanted no part of his plan . . ."

Horne saw that Allen was in pain but he had to learn at least a few details. "How many are there?"

"More than a dozen, sir . . . Sweetwater just joined tonight . . . I was part of it myself . . . But when you came here the other night, sir . . . bringing us tobacco . . . talking about home . . . saying you'd write Ellen a letter for me . . ."

"Save your strength, Allen."

"Sir, McFiddich's dangerous . . . He killed Vega because he didn't like him . . . He hates you too, sir, for some reason I don't—"

Horne saw that Allen was losing blood quickly, that the knife wound had to be staunched.

"Stay quiet, Allen. We'll get Flannery up here to look at you."

The young bare-knuckle fighter winced as he continued. "They've gone to take the *Eclipse*, sir."

Babcock looked at Horne. "Should I get down to the pier and put a few holes in the rowing boat?"

Horne shook his head. "No. They'd know we're onto them. It's better if—" He stopped, staring at a sight beyond the cliffs: a double-masted brig with the flag of France flapping brilliantly in the moonlight.

Seeing the brig approaching on the southern horizon, Horne remembered the mysterious ship which Tyson Lovett had spotted yesterday, the ship which had disappeared beyond the horizon before Horne had arrived with his spyglass. Was it the same one? Were the French keeping Bull Island under surveillance? Were other ships nearby?

Sailing by a westerly breeze, the French brig headed towards the southwest promontory of Bull Island. Horne saw that her larboard gunports were open and that men were swinging from the yardarms, trimming the sails.

Allen temporarily forgot the pain cutting his chest. "Blimey, sir, it's Frenchies!"

Horne's mind moved to the *Eclipse* on the far side of the island.

Babcock asked, "Why are the Frenchies prowling these islands?"

Not answering either man, Horne removed one flintlock from his waistband and laid it on the ground by Allen's leg. "Wait here for Flannery."

Allen shook his head. "Thank you, sir, but don't waste no arms on me."

Babcock rose to his feet. "Take it. If Flannery tries cutting you up when he's drunk, use it on him."

Horne turned to Babcock. "You take the other pistol.

Go to the south ledge. You'll find Midshipman Bruce on Barracks Watch there."

Babcock looked at the weapon. "You trust me a little more now?"

Horne nodded. Babcock's actions had proved his loyalty. Moreover, Horne did not dislike Babcock's straightforward question. The American Colonial was a strong-minded man, not a mewling milktoast who passively took orders.

Tucking the pistol into his waistband, Babcock felt pleased that he had made the decision to reject Mc-Fiddich and stand by Horne. There would be more excitement with the Marines than with any mutineers. Also, Horne had guts. Back in Ohio, men called it 'grit.'

A loud boom exploded across the island.

Allen sat alert against the tree. "What was that?"

"Cannon fire." Horne listened for another report.

Babcock laughed. "If McFiddich took a rowboat out to the *Eclipse*, he's getting more than he bargained for."

Horne heard no second explosion, only the crashing surf. The boom must have been a warning shot fired at the *Eclipse*. If the rumours were true he had heard about France being unable to pay her men wages, the French brig might be prowling among the islands for prizes.

15

True Colours

The brisk wind tossed a silver-capped surf against the island's uneven shoreline, making the water rise in swells around the *Eclipse*. Adam Horne rose and dipped with the swells as he swam towards the frigate, riding a crest to save energy, falling forward into a trough, plunging onwards through the whitecaps.

Swimming from the south, he spotted a jolly-boat bobbing in the surf below the frigate's port entry. McFiddich must have come aboard with a handful of men. He saw, too, that the mutineers had not yet hoisted the anchor lines.

Gripping a tarred anchor line, Horne climbed to the taffrail. He paused before jumping on deck, listening for voices, for footsteps, any noise on the quarterdeck. He raised his head and saw in the moonlight that the main deck milled with men; he looked beyond the larboard bow and spied the white sails of the French brig glistening to the east of the cove's mouth.

Scrambling over the railings, he spotted Pilkington face down on the quarterdeck, the Lieutenant's right hand clenching his sabre, a dark pool of blood spreading from his chest.

Horne fell to the quarterdeck and pressed his ear to Pilkington's back. There was no heart beat.

He wrenched the sabre from Pilkington's grip and remained on his belly as he proceeded fore, straining to make sense of the hubbub of voices below him.

McFiddich was haranguing the crew: "Don't be stupid! I'm your chance for a new life! *Freedom*!"

Horne raised his head cautiously above the carved dowling of the quarterdeck; the moonlight was strong enough for him to spot McFiddich clinging to a ratline, a flintlock in one hand.

"We'll make for Africa! Arabia! Oman! I'll put the port up to a vote!"

A voice called, "How bloody far do you think we'll get with you in command, McFiddich?"

Merlin the gunner pointed towards the cove. "What do you plan to do about them Frenchies out there, McFiddich?"

McFiddich shouted, "They'll help us!"

Scornful laughter met McFiddich's reply, and as further chaos broke out amongst the men, Horne identified faces in the crowd: Tandimmer, Groot, Bakerswell, Jud.

Warnke the purser shouted, "McFiddich, you're going to get us all sent to the gallows!"

Bakerswell the topsman added, "We knew you prison rats would bring us nothing but trouble!"

Ned Wren stepped alongside McFiddich. "Give him

a bloody chance, damn you! He wants to help all of us!"

"Yeah! Help us straight back into prison!"

Tom Gibbons, knife in hand, rushed from the companionway. "Horne's not in his cabin."

McFiddich leapt down from the ratlines. "Look below deck where his pet's locked. In fact, bring up that fancy little Indian—"

A boom from the French brig's cannon roared across the cove; the brig was still out of striking distance but the shot sent the men into further confusion.

Horne knew he must seize the opportunity to act and, deciding to trust a trait he knew in his crew, he remembered an order which every seaman was always ready to obey.

Springing to his feet on the quarterdeck, he shouted, "*Prepare to make way!*"

Silence fell over the main deck. The men stared at Horne as if seeing an apparition.

Horne stabbed Pilkington's sabre towards the mouth of the cove. "That's a French prize crew out there!"

Horne's appearance—his sodden breeches, his bare chest beaded with water, sword high in the moonlight—held the men in a trance.

He singled out Tandimmer. "Cash in on this westerly!"

Next he chose a topsman. "Bakeswell, loose tops'ls!"

He turned to Gibbons. "Heave anchor, bo'sun!"

Knife in hand, Gibbons looked in confusion from

Horne to McFiddich. Captain Horne was trusting him again!

McFiddich raised his pistol, aiming at Horne on the quarterdeck.

Gibbon's stab was fast and he repeated it, pulling out the stained blade from McFiddich's chest as Groot sprung upon Ned Wren, thumbs poking for his jugular vein.

Dropping McFiddich's corpse to deck, Gibbons faced the crew. "Captain Horne's given his orders. So move your lazy arses and heave anchor!"

The bustle became general, men moving to their posts, scurrying up the shrouds, swinging from ratlines, as commands ran through the frigate.

His hands cupped to his mouth, Horne continued shouting orders for all hands on deck, for the anchor to be stowed, gun carriages run out for battle.

16

La Favourite

The Eclipse *caught* the wind, lying over no more than a few degrees, and with an exhilarating lurch, got underway in the moonlight, graceful despite the crew's frenzied work—shrouds singing, fall and block creaking, yards shivering from quick tug and stress.

As the topsails bellied against the starry sky, Horne looked to the mouth of the cove and saw the French brig tacking southeast, bringing her head to the wind as she set a course straight for the *Eclipse*.

Using hands for his trumpet, Horne bellowed, "Set course for northeast!"

"Aye, aye, sir."

"Mind that jib, Groot. The wind's more powerful than you think."

"Aye, aye, *schupper*."

Horne gauged the point in the cove at which the two ships would pass. "Top'ls short!"

Pilkington's body had been carried below deck when

161

Jingee was freed from his irons. No officer stood near Horne to repeat his orders so he shouted above the excited din of the frigate.

"Steer firm, Tandimmer."

"Aye, aye, sir."

"There's tail lag, Gibbons. Get that anchor stowed, blast it!"

Gibbons was thrilled to be once again trusted by his captain and he beat his knotted rope across the back of his tugging crew, exhorting them with a stream of profanities.

Horne tilted back his head. "Jud! Ahoy up there! Any sign of sails beyond?"

The big African waved from his perch high atop the main topgallant mast, signalling to Horne that—as far as moonlight and the surrounding islands allowed a view—there were no other vessels in the night.

The French brig, closing the gap between herself and the *Eclipse*, fired another ball.

The brig was still out of range and Horne interpreted the blast as a ranging shot, wondering if he had mis-read the enemy's intent for a broadside. Might they start firing for the prow? Use their bow-chasers?

He raised his hands to his mouth again and shouted to the gun deck. "Is there time enough and men, Mer-lin, to position a cannon upwards from the waist bat-tery?"

"I'll shoot you the moon, sir!"

"Pack her grape tightly!"

If command aboard the *Eclipse* had previously been slipshod and short of Admiralty standards, the frigate's present activities now defied all naval traditions. But

Horne felt that the men's high spirits compensated for lack of form, that the contact between them was as taut as a violin string, quick as any ship of the line.

"Hoist that cannon to cripple their yards, Merlin!"

"Aye, aye, Captain!"

Horne glanced back at the brig.

Two cables distant, the French ship was still silhouetted on her course to pass a'beam the *Eclipse*.

Checking Merlin's progress with the cannon, Horne spied Jingee running along the gangway, scurrying with a succession of wooden buckets, alternating loads of sand and water—sand to give grip to the gunners' feet, water for drenching sudden fires.

The sound of the French brig drew his attention back to battle. The distance between the two ships was shortening as they continued on a parallel course, their prows closing . . .

"Prepare to—"

Horne waited another one, two, three seconds . . .

"—*fire*!"

The cannons belched flames, blue clouds of smoke rising in the night. Both ships shook under the impact. The acrid odour of gunpowder filled the air.

Feeling the deck tremble beneath his bare feet, Horne heard timbers crash, sails rip, the screams of men rising from the gun deck.

The two ships continued past one another, their timbers groaning like two crippled leviathans, leaving wisps of smoke in their wake.

Craning his neck to inspect the damage done to the *Eclipse*'s yards or masts, Horne was pleased to see that the crashing sound had not come from the frigate. He turned to evaluate the damage done to the French brig and saw her topgallant and topsails crashing downwards, the canvas twisting like wings of a moth singed by a flame. Merlin had struck his target.

Lowering his eyes to the brig's stern, he saw that the French ship followed the new naval fashion of wearing her name resplendent in gilt paint—*La Favourite*.

Another cannon explosion rent the air and Horne jerked his head, wondering if he had missed a manoeuvre. Across the portside stern, he saw the island's stone pier explode in the moonlight.

La Favourite was firing on the settlement.

Headquarters was a powderkeg, the stone house filled with ammunition and explosives. Before Horne could think of a way to warn Rajit, Babcock, and Mercer's watch to evacuate to the far side of the island, he heard another burst of fire and saw that a warning was too late—Headquarters exploded in a cloud of white smoke.

The bastards!

The crew's anger matched Horne's, and as their curses rose from deck, Horne trumpeted, "Stand by to go about!"

The men needed no urging.

Tandimmer let the spokes of the wheel spin through his hands.

"Head to wind!"

"Aye, aye, sir!"

Sails thundered; canvas snapped; the yards ran alive

with the quick figures of the crew and prisoners doubling as seamen.

The *Eclipse* caught her stays. But the movements were not fast enough for Horne's liking, and he bellowed, "Get it over, men! Hang her up in that wind!"

Ropes screamed, blocks groaned, and as the *Eclipse* spun in the night, water swelled, creaming from the frigate's prow, bubbling in her wake.

"Prepare to fire!"

"Guns sponged and loaded, sir."

"Canister on round shot?"

"Aye, aye, sir."

The *Eclipse* turned in the mouth of the cove, moving on the course blazed by *La Favourite*. Seeing the French brig presently tacking and preparing to come back for the *Eclipse*, Horne nodded to himself as he watched her bringing her stern to the wind. He was pleased to see the ship move awkwardly in the manoeuvre.

As his next plan boiled in his brain, he again began gauging at what point the two ships would come a'beam one another. He only had a few minutes for preparations.

"Seize grappling hooks!"

No more than a few men at first understood his plan.

"Seize grappling hooks and form three boarding parties!"

A cheer spread through the decks as more and more men grabbed the spiked irons attached to long throwing ropes.

Horne commanded, "Board the enemy to capture, not to kill!"

Now everyone understood that Horne was ordering hand-to-hand battle.

"I repeat—do not board to kill. Board to take the ship as a prize, not the enemy as corpses!"

Horne pointed Pilkington's sabre. "Lovett, board men from the prow."

"Yes, sir."

"Bapu, you lead from amidship."

The Rajasthani bandit raised his fist in agreement. "Yes, sir!"

"I will lead from the stern. But we wait for the brig to come astern."

Horne raised the sabre above his head. "Now arm yourselves!"

Not knowing how many men he had aboard the *Eclipse*, he guessed that the French crew would easily outnumber them two to one. He could only depend on his men's enthusiasm and the physical training they had received in the past few days.

"Cannon ready?"

"Aye, aye, sir."

"Weapons to hand?"

His answer was a roar.

Horne thought of the nickname tagged to Bombay Marines. They *did* look like a shipful of buccaneers, himself included.

He smiled for the first time in—how long had it been since he had smiled so proudly?

Armed with Pilkington's sabre, a dirk in his other hand and a flintlock stuck into his waistband, Horne felt the wind against his naked chest as he clung to the ratlines and watched the two ships drawing closer for their second encounter. He listened to timbers creaking, sails snapping, waves slapping against their hulls as he waited for the best moment to order—"Fire!"

Cannon smoke engulfed the two ships.

"Throw grappling hooks!"

The spikes flew towards the brig like iron stars. The men began tugging the ropes as the topsmen descended the ratlines and shrouds, their whoops filling the night.

Horne waited for the two bulwarks to collide.

"Board!"

Leaping over the railing, he led his men across the narrow gap, stabbing his dirk towards a swarthy sailor who greeted him with the swing of an axe.

A French officer, natty in gold braid, hurried to form a line of Marines to repulse the boarding party. But the soldiers were too excited, fumbling as they poured shot into their muzzles.

Horne dodged a strike from a spiked club and continued fore, stabbing to slice a pistol butt from an officer's hand. All around him the deck was filled with the clank of steel and the pop, pop, pop of flintlocks.

Seeing that the French resistance was weakening quickly, no match for his men's ferocity, Horne reached the brig's most vital spot and swung his sabre with both hands, sinking the blade into the rope which held the French colours to the mast.

The flag fluttered downwards, cheers arising from Horne's men as *La Favourite* became a prize for the Bombay Marine.

17

The Ceremony

Commodore Watson brushed the yellow dust from his frockcoat after inspecting the damage done to Bull Island. "You made yourself a compact little drill station here, Horne. Too bad old Frenchie had to come along and blast it to smithereens."

Less than twenty-four hours had passed since *La Favourite* had begun firing on the *Eclipse*. Even less time had elapsed since Commodore Watson had arrived in his flagship, *Ferocious*, forty-two guns, announcing to Adam Horne that he had brought important news from Bombay Castle. So far Watson had not divulged the reason why he had appeared two weeks ahead of schedule.

Adam Horne had not changed clothes since Jud had spotted the *Ferocious* billowing against the purpling of the new dawn; the time since then had been spent dividing the French prisoners between the *Eclipse*, *La Favourite*, and the one shore Barracks which had been quickly transformed into a gaol. After interviewing the French captain, a shrewish man named Pierre Tolent, Horne had conducted burial services for his casualties, committing their death hammocks to the sea before heat hastened putrefaction.

Commodore Watson shaded his eyes in the glare of the midday sun as he faced Horne in the harbour yard. "Some officers have a genius for handling vast numbers of men, Horne. Your gift appears to be surviving with damned few."

Horne had lost five men aboard the *Eclipse* during last night's battle and two more from the land explosion. Among them had been two prisoners he had never come to know, Jim Pugh and Edward Quinte. He added the deaths of McFiddich and Wren to the toll, as well as their killing of Vega and the demise this morning of Martin Allen from his knife wound. He had lost a total of eleven men—prisoners, crew, Marines—nine of them having belonged to the special squad he had been training.

"I make do, sir."

Watson glanced towards the *Eclipse* anchored on the lee side of *La Favourite*. "Your crew must be near enough depleted, Horne."

"By many men's standards, sir, yes."

Unlike Horne, Watson felt strangely lighthearted. He was pleased to be away from the pressures of Bombay Castle. Also, he did not have to worry about his wife discovering that he had broken his abstinence from spirits.

"I propose, Horne, that we reward the officer who

evacuated the men from your Headquarters before Frenchie began gunning it."

"The man's not an officer, sir. He's one of the prisoners."

Watson's porcine eyes widened. "A prisoner?"

"Yes, sir. His name's Fred Babcock. He carried Marine Sergeant Rajit on his back to the top of that plateau."

Watson looked from the plateau back to Horne.

"So you only have two officers now?"

"Correct, sir. Midshipman Bruce and Midshipman Mercer. We read Last Rites over Lieutenant Pilkington at dawn. I shall be writing to his family this evening."

Watson considered the situation. "Horne, take time today to provide me with the names of men you'd like promoted at tonight's ceremony."

"Ceremony, sir?"

"The induction of your new Marines."

Horne did not understand. "Sir, I thought you would induct the new men officially after the mission."

"I think they proved themselves worthy to be Marines, Horne."

Horne felt his first moment of elation for the day. "Yes, sir. Thank you, sir."

Studying Horne's unshaven face, the stubble of which was only a fraction shorter than the dark bristles on his shaved head, Watson said, "Horne, I'm surprised you haven't asked why I arrived a fortnight ahead of schedule."

"Sir, if seven years in service to the Honourable East India Company has taught me anything, it's to prepare myself for the worst."

"And what, Horne, would be the worst at this moment?"

"The Governors have advanced the mission, sir. We're to leave immediately for Fort St. George."

Watson put his arm around Horne's shoulders, then remembering that he was covered with perspiration and grime, he quickly pulled away, saying, "Horne, why not come aboard the *Ferocious* with me now? The awning will be stretched across the quarterdeck. We can sit in the shade. Have a gin. I can tell you the few things I've learnt about the assignment since I last saw you."

Horne recognized the invitation as a command.

"Yes, sir."

Following Watson down to the jolly-boat, he glanced at the heap of rubble and stones which had once been Headquarters. Was his stay at Bull Island already over? Had his work here been profitable?

In the evening ceremony conducted aboard the *Ferocious*, Commodore Watson raised Midshipman Bruce and Midshipman Mercer to Second and Third Lieutenant respectively. Their age differences and lengths of service in the Honourable East India Company influenced their promotions in rank.

Adam Horne recommended three crew members to be raised to Midshipman—George Tandimmer, Corin Bramhall, Chris Bennett—a temporary step to make them higher commissioned officers. But Tandimmer declined the honour, saying he hoped to retire early to an uncle's farm in Dorset. Horne doubted the existence of such an uncle or farm while admiring Tandimmer's refusal to rise above a station he enjoyed aboard the *Eclipse*. Bramhall and Bennett both eagerly accepted the offer to swear their oaths to King and Company, as well as to be eligible to receive four pounds boost in pay per annum.

The shipboard ceremony also included the Marine induction. Seven men remained from the original sixteen prisoners from Bombay Castle—Babcock, Bapu, Groot, Kiro, Jingee, Jud and Mustafa.

All the men had been amongst Horne's final contenders, except for Jingee who had been locked in the ship's hold. The duel with McFiddich had proved that Jingee had the ability to fight. His actions during the battle with *La Favourite* had shown his loyalty. Instead of punishing him for fighting with McFiddich, Horne gave him the choice of becoming a Marine.

The squadron would consist only of prisoners from Bombay Castle. Had that been his hidden wish all along? Horne wondered.

The sinking sun painted the evening sky a lush spectrum of rose and purple, a slight breeze flapping the quarterdeck's awning as Commodore Watson seized an opportunity after administering the Oaths of Allegiance to deliver a few words to the assembled men.

"Despite the way Captain Horne has pampered you in the past weeks, the life of a Bombay Marine is not the party you've been enjoying on Bull Island."

Polite laughter greeted Watson's joke, the seven new Marines still uneasy in the broadcloth uniforms hurriedly provided for them from the flagship's stores.

Cheeks red from an afternoon spent drinking gin and

lemon juice, Watson expounded on the fame of his predecessor, Commodore William James, before airing his repertoire, of humour about "the other Watson," Rear Admiral of the Red Charles Watson, with whom people still confused him, despite the fact that Charles Watson had died four years ago.

Adam Horne's mind wandered during Watson's tipsy speech-making, remembering the facts he had been given that afternoon about the decision of the three Governors to send the Marine squadron earlier than scheduled into Fort St. George. As he had guessed, the assignment to Madras *was* to abduct the French Commander-in-Chief, General Thomas Lally. But Watson had refused to expound this afternoon on the reasons for the action. He dwelled on the difficulties to expect inside the fortress, explaining that the Marines must treat the British Army and Navy as enemy.

Laughter jolted Horne back to the present.

Expansively, Watson was announcing, "We shall sail in convoy at tomorrow's dawn for the Coromandel Coast. Captain Horne will disembark with you seven new men near Cuddalore. Horne's planning a spot more shore training."

The announcement surprised Horne. Should Watson be disclosing such a detail so publicly?

Watson continued, "From Cuddalore, we'll proceed north with *La Favourite* for Bengal where you can lay claim to your prize money. Ten per cent of that brig divided amongst you will buy a few bobs' worth of pudding, eh?"

Cheers and whistles spread across deck.

"Now I want every man to enjoy himself with the refreshments provided. But remember—we sail at dawn!"

As the seamen and Marines began to disperse, Horne looked for his escape from the flagship. Sergeant Rajit had been left in command of Barracks Prison Detail and Horne wanted to talk to him, to prepare him for his exclusion from the mission.

Feeling an arm on his shoulder, his heart sank. He expected to turn and find Watson pressing a gin into his hand.

Instead, he saw Babcock.

"What's this about 'shore-training'?"

The brash question startled Horne. He had not planned to explain the mission to the squad until they were aboard the *Eclipse* and bound for the Coromandel Coast.

Babcock's hair had grown long enough to part down the middle of his forehead, making his ears look more prominent.

"That's why you chose us from prison, isn't it? For some secret mission?"

Horne's first reaction was to discipline Babcock for insolence and for failing again to address an officer properly, but not wanting to alert the other men to the American's astute guess, he checked the impulse and said, "Babcock, for someone so badly disciplined, you sometimes show surprising intelligence."

Babcock pulled one ear. "Is that some kind of compliment . . . sir?"

"Only for tonight, Babcock. And another thing."

Babcock blinked.

"Keep your suspicions to yourself."

Turning, Horne moved quickly towards the port entry, realising that Elihu Cornhill had taught him how to escape from everything but a social gathering aboard a Commodore's flagship.

Fort St. George was a fortress within a fortress, the Honourable East India Company's most important settlement on India's eastern coast, in the Presidency of Madras. The Military Guardhouse and King's Army Barracks formed the western wall of the outer fortress, stretching between the Nabob's Bastion on the southwest to the Royal Bastion on the northeast.

Inside the Guardhouse a man was imprisoned in a small, humid room; he sat on the edge of a cot, his head bent forward, his hands clasped between the thighs of his white breeches. European, fifty-six years old, he was attired in a clean shirt, his white hair knotted at the nape of his sunburnt neck. He appeared to be agitated, constantly fidgeting with his hands.

Springing from the cot, he paced the room's plank floor, glowering at the four cracked plaster walls of the prison.

A wooden crucifix hung above the cot; a deal table and rattan-bottomed chair were positioned against the opposite wall; the table held writing materials and three leather-bound volumes, one of the books being a Roman Catholic breviary inscribed by the man's confessor and friend, *Père* Lavour. To the man, this room was as desolate as Madras itself.

He had always thought poorly of Madras, even when he had besieged Fort St. George two years ago, leading an army of three thousand European horse and foot soldiers, five hundred native cavalrymen and three thousand Sepoys.

Oh, the fickleness of fate!

Here he was back in Madras, a prisoner, and not even accommodated according to his rank.

What liars these English were! What had happened to the terms of the capitulation which the English officers had so greedily signed? The requirements for civilized treatment? A bountiful table and adequate drink and a garden for reflection? How long would he be kept in this cell—in bleak Fort St. George—before being taken to England as his captors had agreed? He wondered now if Colonel Eyre Coote was trying to renege on the terms of surrender as he had also been so ready to exclude Admiral Pocock from the victory at Pondicherry?

The man continued pacing the floor, planning how he might spring upon the next man who stepped through the door. Not a wretched servant but some man of consequence who *must* soon call upon him. He considered what weapon he would use: a leg from the table or chair; a string of rattan for a garrotte; any improvised weapon to show that he was still a man to be reckoned with—a soldier, a leader.

His eyes stopped on the wall crucifix. Pulling it from its peg, he gripped the small wooden cross by its base, cutting it down through the air, chopping with the crossarms of the crucifix as if it were an axe.

Smiling, he resumed his pacing of the room, remembering words from his Jesuit education in Paris—*Ad*

Majorem Dei Gloriam. The crucifix made a good, sharp little weapon. And if not for the Greater Glory of God, then at least for the glory—and survival—of Thomas Lally, Baron de Tolendahl.

PART THREE
Into The Fortress

18

The Convoy

The **Eclipse,** *the* *Ferocious* and the captured *La Favourite*, manned by a prize crew from Watson's flagship, weighed anchor at the light of the new day, sailing south from Bull Island, enjoying a strong westerly through the Laccadives, the Maldives, and on past Minicoy. Avoiding the Gulf of Mannar with its treacherous reefs, the convoy rode the sea winds around Ceylon, the southern tip of India, and climbed the Bay of Bengal towards the Coromandel Coast.

Aboard the *Eclipse*, Adam Horne continued preparing the seven newly-inducted Bombay Marines. He had divided the men, along with himself, into two groups, Land Group and Sea Group, and today he worked inside his cabin with them, reviewing the steps they were to follow after landing south of Madras.

Horne sat on the edge of his desk, one boot crossed over the other, arms folded across his chest. "Land Group is Babcock, Bapu, Groot and Mustafa. Sea

Group consists of Kiro, Jingee, Jud and myself. After
landing, Land Group heads for the village of Sharuna.
Sea Group goes up the coast to Attur. We do not meet
again until we are inside the fortress, so we must know
each other's movements thoroughly."

The seven men squatted or lay around Horne's
cabin, the four men of Land Group ranged near the
berth, the three men travelling with Horne in Sea
Group sitting facing the desk.

Poorly disciplined; loud mouthed; quick tempered or
sour faced. Each man had his fault, but each was also
physically able, mentally alert, willing to take chances.
If anybody could kidnap General Lally from the Army
Guardhouse, Horne was certain his oddly matched
squadron of ex-prisoners could do it.

Satisfied with the men, he did not begrudge them
the long hours it took to review details about Fort St.
George and the surrounding land. Keen with excitement, his few nightly hours of sleep were frequently
broken by new ideas—or refinements of old ones—for
abducting the French Commander-in-Chief.

Despite the long hours of work, he was relaxed and
content. Sitting on the edge of his desk, he continued,
"I considered using local fishermen to support Sea
Group in catamarans but decided against it. We must
trust nobody outside our two groups."

Jud—assigned to Sea Group—raised his arm, the
skin darkened to a blue-blackness by the sun.

Horne nodded permission to speak.

"Sir, you said that the boat we'll get from Attur will
be a sewn boat."

"Board sewn with rope, Jud. The local name is *masulah*."

"I should have told you before, sir, I sailed rope boats in Oman."

"There's probably a difference, Jud. Madras boats are known to be top heavy. They capsize easily in the surf—but not as easily as most boats."

Kiro raised his hand.

"Kiro."

"They sound like Nagasaki fishing boats, Captain. Two men can keep them afloat."

"Let's hope so, Kiro. Jingee tells me his cousins in Attur will give us a *masulah*. But we'll take anything that can float if we get desperate."

Horne resumed his briefing. "The main gate of Fort St. George faces the sea. It's called the Sea Gate. There's a drawbridge, a moat, two dry ditches and a gate. The drawbridge is seldom hoisted and the gate's manned twenty-four hours a day. Everyone who enters or leaves through the Sea Gate is logged into a ledger."

Kiro again raised his hand. The Japanese had become easier and more relaxed since Horne had discovered the reason why he had been so hesitant about striking opponents in the drills. Horne had instructed the men not to take any lives during the mission but, not wanting Kiro to hesitate to use *Karate* in silencing anyone trying to hinder their success, he had included him in Sea Group, so that he could use Kiro's *Karate* along with his own *Pankration*.

Kiro pointed at the lantern swinging from the cabin's wooden beam. "Captain, if it's night-time when we reach the fort, how do we see if there's no moon?"

Horne recrossed his arms. "Street lamps were installed last year in Fort St. George. They burn coconut oil and are covered with glass globes. The Sea Gate is equipped with three coconut oil lamps. That's another reason for us to avoid entering there."

A hand was raised from the cot.

"Babcock."

"What if Land Group's inside the fort and Sea Group don't show up?"

Horne turned the question to test Babcock's memory of past sessions. "Where does Land Group first look for Sea Group?"

"Nabob's Bastion."

"Locate it for me, Babcock."

Babcock tried to picture the ground plan of Fort St. George which Horne had made the men memorize the first morning after leaving Bull Island.

"Nabob's Bastion is at—" Babcock's memory cleared, "—the southwest corner of the Sea Wall."

"And if Sea Group is not below Nabob's Bastion, Babcock, where do you look for us?"

"St. Thomas Bastion, southeast corner."

"So what's your question, Babcock?"

"If you don't turn up?"

"Just wait. Patiently. Without Sea Group, Land Group must not proceed. The same holds in reverse. You get us in. We all get Lally out. We can't both go through the gates because, unfortunately, somebody might recognize me. There must be no possibility of tracing Lally's disappearance to the Bombay Marine."

Babcock was the only man who had asked Horne why the assignment was to kidnap a French general from the British Army. Horne had answered that a Marine's job was to obey orders, not to ask for reasons, and in the last few days Thomas Lally's name had become as familiar to the seven men as their own, without anybody asking for further explanations.

Looking around the cabin, Horne asked, "More questions about the fort? Garrison details? Army barracks? Company Barracks?"

Silence filled the cabin, broken only by the sound of the *Eclipse* sailing under full canvas, the toss and fall of the frigate enjoying the strong winds.

"No questions about the Guard House? Portuguese Square? The Stable?"

Outside the cabin, the call of Lieutenant Bruce's voice marked the change of the second watch.

"You think you know everything?"

Bapu raised his hand. "I've got a question about the Bazaar, Captain."

Horne was surprised how well the broad-shouldered Indian, Bapu, obeyed his orders. He had prepared himself for serious insubordination from a man who had once led a gang of hill bandits. But since the early days of the voyage when Bapu had shot the two swimmers escaping from the *Eclipse*, he had been one of Horne's best disciplined men. Bapu's only fault was that he was a slow learner.

"Sir, what if the Bazaar's closed when Land Group reaches the Black Town? What's our cover then?"

"Bapu, do you remember the name of the gate on the North Wall?"

Bapu scratched the prickly burr of his head. "On the North Wall?"

"Yes, Bapu, the North Wall," Horne answered patiently. He had learnt that it was best to speak to Bapu as if he were a child, albeit a big one.

"Is it the Main Gate?"

"Correct, Bapu. The Main Gate. And like the Sea Gate on the opposite wall, guard outside the Main Gate is posted twenty-four hours a day."

"Sir, are there street lamps at the Main Gate?"

"Two. And don't forget, Bapu, the Main Gate is also the busiest entry into Fort St. George. There's activity night as well as day. Land Group shouldn't make anybody suspicious even if the Bazaar is closed—providing that you wear the disguises you'll be carrying and remember to follow your instructions."

Horne repositioned himself on the edge of the desk. "If you *need* cover, Bapu, always create a diversion."

Horne looked from Bapu sitting on the mattress to Mustafa, Babcock and Dirk Groot squatting in front of him on deck. Studying the four men of Land Group, he said, "Before we review our plans for inside the walls, are there any more questions about the approach?"

Silence.

He looked at the men facing the desk. "Sea Group?"

Confidence.

Moving his eyes back to the berth, Horne considered a hypothetical situation for Land Group. "What if you're nearing the fortress and a British patrol stops you at Elambore. First of all, where's Elambore?"

Groot raised his hand. "The settlement of Elambore, *schupper*, is southwest of Madras. Up on the plain by the old Muslim Tollgate."

"Correct. Now how do you identify yourself to the British Patrol?"

Babcock raised his hand and Horne nodded.

"Didn't you tell us that the French surrendered Pondicherry last month?"

Horne nodded again, having given the men the details which Watson had told him.

Babcock sat with his arms crossing his bent knees. "And isn't Pondicherry only a couple of days south of Madras?"

"About three days."

"So if we meet a patrol, Groot here keeps his '*aye, aye, schupper*' mouth shut and lets me do the talking. I say to the patrol that we're stragglers from the fighting down at that Pondicherry place."

Horne decided that this was not the time to reprimand Babcock for failing again to address an officer correctly. Instead, he asked, "What do you say to the patrol, Babcock, if they ask you the name of your company?"

"79th Foot."

"Who's your commanding officer?"

Babcock pulled on his ear. "If they ask me too many details like that, I suddenly get heat stroke or belly cramps."

"Good but not good enough."

Horne reached behind him on the desk for the list of regiments he had received from Watson. Apart from schedules, names and details about Fort St. George, he had also been supplied with a wide assortment of uniforms and clothes for the men to pack with their equipment.

Dropping the list back onto the desk, he said, "If you belong to the 79th Foot, Babcock, your commanding officer is Pilfer. Can you remember that?"

"Pilfer? Who could forget it? It's like 'pilchards.' I hate 'em."

"It also means 'to steal,' Babcock."

"Then I've got *two* good reasons to remember."

Laughter filled the cabin. But Horne called for order, knowing there were many facts to review between now and the time when the *Eclipse* would drop them in an open boat off the inlet on the Chingleput coastline.

"Now, men, let's suppose we're inside the fortress. But before we move onto details about General Lally, let's run through a few local facts."

He looked at Jingee who had become his model Marine, as well as the chief informant on the ways of Tamil Indians living along the Coromandel Coast. The only problem Horne had with Jingee was keeping him from spending his time cooking, cleaning and pressing clothes.

"Who's in charge of Fort St. George when Governor Pigot's away?"

"The Town Major, Captain sahib."

"Is the Town Major a military or Company officer?"

"Company, sahib. The post of Town Major was created two years ago by Governor Pigot."

Horne looked at Jud squatting next to Jingee on deck, an ebony giant beside a chocolate gremlin.

"Jud, if you go to the Portuguese Church, what religion are you?"

Jud blessed himself with the sign of the cross.

"But are services held there?"

"No, sir. The Company's redesigning the Portuguese Church. Catholics now go to services in the Armenian Church outside the walls."

Horne looked over to Land Group. "Mustafa, what if you're standing outside the Main Gate and you hear a church bell. Where's it coming from?"

"The English Church, Captain. Church bells begin ringing at six in the morning. We listen to them for our escape signals."

Horne had more to worry about at the moment than why Mustafa seldom talked and *never* smiled. He pressed on with the questions.

The wind held strong, warming with the Bengalese Current as the convoy moved up the western perimeter of the Bay of Bengal. Commodore Watson stood on the quarterdeck of the *Ferocious* in the light of the new day, the low hills of the Chingleput Range rising above the rocky coastline beyond the larboard. Adam Horne would be taking his men ashore in less than an hour.

Lifting a silver flask to his mouth, Watson felt the liquor burn his throat, reminding him of Tim Flannery. Adam Horne was displeased that he had to take Flannery ashore with his squadron.

Flannery was an old friend of Watson's, a drinking companion from Spithead and Gravesend and Deptford. Watson had assigned Flannery to the *Eclipse* after the British Navy had discharged him in Bombay. Sending him ashore with Horne's squadron was a precaution Watson was taking in case Lally were injured in the escape and needed medical attention. Lally was Irish himself—at least, half-Irish—and Watson hoped that Flannery might also amuse the temperamental prisoner with a bit of dry Celtic wit.

Looking through his spyglass, Watson studied the bellying topsails of the *Eclipse*. After the frigate had landed Horne's team, she would follow the *Ferocious* and *La Favourite* to sea, the three ships beginning their wait for Horne to return to the same spot with Lally. The wait would last anywhere from one to two days. If Horne did not return in forty-eight hours, the convoy would weigh anchor and Horne's mission would be counted as lost.

Watson had decided against telling Horne that the Company's three Governors were threatening to disband the Bombay Marine if the mission failed. Horne had enough to worry about with the French—as well as the English—as his enemy.

Admiral Pocock was prowling the Bay with the Navy, and Watson had also cautioned Horne to be prepared for d'Ache's fleet. But Pocock's presence off Madras should keep the French at a safe distance. The only threat from the French was likely to be from their land troops.

Hoisting the flask to his mouth, Watson took another long swig but did not enjoy it. The liquor's potency no longer affected him, barely numbing his nerves. He reflected how bitterly disappointed Emma would be by his breaking of his abstinence, but it was drink, he recalled, that had helped him set out from Bombay Castle. It was damned hard for an officer to be true both to his wife and to a tough command.

Feeling the seaspray against his face, he stared blankly across the choppy waves at the *Eclipse*, wondering if Adam Horne had reached that state of life, where he could be true only to his mission and his orders. Such dedication took some officers many years to reach. Some called it an achievement. Others, self-ishness. Had Horne come that far yet, or did he still believe that a man could hope to have home, family life and happiness on shore?

People had been saying for hundreds of years that the sea was a lonely place. It was true. The damned sea took its toll on a man. Especially when you sailed for a Company concerned only with profits.

Adam Horne had changed in some ways, though. Watson had noticed it on Bull Island. Overworked. Undermanned. Pressed for time. Nevertheless Horne seemed more exhilarated, less nervous than he had in Bombay Castle. Was it because he was coming closer to action? About to embark on an adventure that would turn most men's bowels to water? Watson considered how he himself now felt dulled, made blunt by alcohol. He could not help but feel jealous.

Stuffy chambers. Long meetings. Disappointments. It was hell getting old, using gin to cope with pressures.

19

The Coromandel Coast

The water was brilliant and translucent off the Coromandel Coast, more green than blue, with meandering shapes of jagged coral reefs visible through a gently rippling tide. Long weed trailed down to the great depths of the inlet, and oddly shaped fish swam close to the surface, unafraid of the small boat with its eight oars rising and dipping in unison.

Adam Horne crouched in the snub prow of the boat, listening to the creak of the oars in the rowlocks as the boat moved away from the *Eclipse*. The terrain ahead appeared exactly as Jingee had described—low mountains covered with brambles, scrub brush, small copses of pine, a few stunted palms.

The keel touched sand. Horne and Mustafa jumped into the lapping surf and pulled the boat onto the beach as the other six men left the oars to gather their weapons and packs of equipment.

Tim Flannery, a wide-brimmed straw hat pulled

down over his head, rose from the stern bench. "Look, a hut!"

The shout echoed in the cove's silence, broken only by the chirrup of crickets and the gentle lap of the surf onto the crescent of golden sand.

The hut's presence told Horne that they had come ashore at the correct spot. He hoped Jingee had been equally accurate in describing the roads and distances they would travel from here.

The men worked quickly, heaping a pile of equipment on the sand, beaching the boat, carrying the oars to the hut where Flannery would be lodging while he waited for them to return with Lally.

Horne pointed towards a small peninsula separating the sandy inlet from a lagoon. "There's a good spot to weather the boat."

Jud and Kiro grabbed the boat between them and walked towards the escarpment, their bare heels sinking into the soggy yellow sand.

Horne scrambled up the black rocks. He saw that the lagoon darkened to a deeper blue beyond the shore. The *Eclipse* could safely take refuge there when they returned for the rendezvous. The thought of Bruce and Mercer being in command of the frigate troubled him. He turned, blanking it from his mind.

As the men worked to cover the boat with dried brush and reeds, Horne moved back to the beach and selected a flintlock, a musket and a bag of shot from the pile. Then he continued towards the hut where Flannery was collecting dried palms for the roofless shelter. "No more than a garden shed, now is it?" commented the Irishman.

"Hmmm." Horne noticed two large bottles of spirits and wondered how Watson hoped that Flannery would remain sober enough to help Lally if there were an accident during the escape.

Setting down the weapons and ammunition by the rattan-covered bottles, he said brusquely, "You're to use these to protect the boat if necessary, Mr. Flannery."

Flannery placed another palm frond on the shelter. "And not to guard myself, Captain?"

"If need be, Mr. Flannery."

"How about using them for a bit of hunting? This land's got some fat little turtledoves."

"We'll be back in two days. You have more than enough food to last you until then. It won't be necessary to hunt *or* to build fires, Mr. Flannery."

Flannery studied Horne. "You're a hard man, aren't you, Adam Horne. Hard on your men as well as hard on yourself."

"I have a job to do, Mr Flannery, as you have."

Flannery's eyes twinkled. "Aye, Captain."

Horne disliked the Irishman's mocking stare. "Mr Flannery, the custom of saying two 'ayes' when answering a Captain has a definite purpose. It informs him that you understand orders. Do *you* understand your orders, Mr Flannery?"

Flannery's thin lips twisted into a smile. "Aye, aye, Captain Horne."

"Good. I expect them to be obeyed." Horne turned back to his men.

•   •   •

Tim Flannery finished the repairs to the hut, unpacked his food supply and damned a small pool for cooling his water jug, not forgetting to make a cache for his rum. The work occupied him until Horne and the men departed in two groups, each party going in opposite directions.

Alone on the beach, Flannery hunted in vain for his straw hat, so knotting a cloth on his head as the Marines had done on Bull Island, he settled himself against a rotting log, his bare feet buried in the sand and a rum bottle nestling between his thighs.

Enjoying the sun glittering on the slightly ruffled surf, he said aloud, "Oh, this is a grand life, old Flannery."

His words sounded empty in the abandoned cove.

"A grand life for an old codger like you."

He remembered Commodore Watson's promise to secure him a position as surgeon on shore as repayment for taking part in this operation. Such a plum assignment would give Flannery a retirement pension, a rosy old age paid for by the Honourable East India Company. He took a swig from the rattan-covered bottle, picturing to himself the thatched cottage he would buy back home in Kilkelly. He could retire comfortably to County Mayo on a surgeon's pension.

But a surgeon's post in Bombay or Madras, or even Calcutta, might mean forsaking the oath Flannery had sworn sixteen years ago, the pledge to avenge his brother's murder. Was a pension worth forgetting that promise? He took another drink from the bottle, telling himself not to rush a decision; liquor dripped down his chin and onto his chest. Flannery began to warble a stanza of *The White Cockade*, the anthem sung by the Irishmen serving in France under Thomas Lally back in '44–45. Flannery's brother had belonged to that infantry of mercenaries known as the Wild Geese. Padraic Flannery had been killed serving under Lally on the fields of Fontenoy on 11 May, 1745.

20
The Donkey Cart

LAND GROUP

Two miles inland from the Chingleput coastline lay the small village of Sharuna, a cluster of straw-roofed huts, a walled Hindu temple and a reservoir with stone steps descending into its murky green water. The land looked like the rest of the District of Arcot: desolate, sun-baked, dotted with leafless trees making grotesque shapes against a cloudless blue sky.

The dirt track leading to Sharuna was bordered on one side by a deep ditch and a thicket of thorns dense enough to give cover to Babcock, Groot and Mustafa, as they waited for Bapu to return from the village with transport for the rest of the journey to Fort St. George. Horne had given orders for the squadron's two Indians, Bapu and Jingee, to act as spokesmen for Land Group and Sea Group when necessary.

Groot lay on his belly in the ditch, his eyes fixed on

the rise in the road. "What's taking him so long?" he kept asking anxiously.

Babcock lounged on the incline, his head propped on his canvas pack, the straw hat he had stolen from Flannery pulled down over his eyes. Mustafa sat a short distance away, his back against a pine-tree, a glum expression on his broad chiselled face as he idly pulled on the wing of a brown grasshopper.

Of Land Group, Groot appeared to be the most enthusiastic about the mission, his enthusiasm approaching nervousness. But even he had not been able to offer an explanation for the assignment.

He had raised the matter again as Land Group had hiked from the inlet. "If General Lally surrendered to the British, the French are probably frightened he's going to give away all their war secrets."

Trudging in front of Groot up the dusty track, Babcock had disagreed. "That's no reason why the Company's Marine has to kidnap him from a British prison."

"Yah. You're right." Groot had kept on hiking.

Two hours later, Groot still had not thought of a satisfactory answer and meanwhile Bapu had gone to the village to find an animal for travelling.

"Do you think he's run into trouble?" he asked nervously, looking down the road.

Babcock flicked his hand at a fly as he lay on the slope. "You worry too much, Groot."

Groot squinted beneath the brim of the blue cap pulled down over his pale blond eyebrows. "I got reason to worry, maybe. The Tamils don't like people from the North and Bapu's from the North."

"What about Jingee? He's a Tamil and he and Bapu get along fine."

Groot considered Babcock's argument.

Snapping his big fist at the persistent fly, Babcock added, "I tell you, don't worry. Bapu's probably been spotted by some girl he'd promised to come back and marry."

"Marry?" Groot glanced at Babcock relaxed in the ditch. "Bapu's got a girl here?"

Babcock frowned. Why did this fidgety Dutchman never understand his jokes?

But Mustafa, his back to the pine-tree, agreed with a grunt as he pulled off the grasshopper's other wing.

Babcock lifted the straw hat off his face. Groot also looked at Mustafa. It was rare to hear him make any noise, or to communicate in any way with the other men.

Nodding his big square head, Mustafa said, "There's girls waiting to catch *me* back in Alanya."

"Back where?" Babcock sat up and studied the Turk.

"Alanya. My home."

"And you've got a girl there?" Babcock shot an amused look at Groot.

"Many, many girls."

Babcock pulled his ear. "Some ugly big pig like you's got a girl?"

Mustafa's dark eyes hardened as he glared at Babcock.

Babcock did not want to fight Mustafa over some senseless remark. But he did want to know more about this sullen Turk and, grinning, he pressed, "Come on, tell us something, man."

"Tell you—" Mustafa jerked a leg from the grass-hopper, "—what?"

"About your girl. Home. Yourself."

Mustafa looked suspiciously from Babcock to Groot. "Why you two want to know about me? Who you going to tell about me?"

"Nobody. But if we're going to be together . . ."

Groot waved his hand for Babcock and Mustafa to be silent. "Somebody's coming."

Babcock listened, hearing in the distance a rattling sound accompanied by an odd, eerie wail.

The rattling grew louder on the far side of the rise in the dusty road. Babcock, Groot, and Mustafa lay on their bellies in the ditch, listening to what sounded like somebody singing in a high-pitched voice, a song rhythmless to their ears.

A small black donkey and a two-wheeled cart appeared over the hill, a peasant sitting slumped high on the cart's bench with a soiled white mantle wrapped around his head and shoulders.

Groot whispered. "Farmer."

Babcock glanced in the opposite direction. "Let's ambush him for the cart."

Mustafa grunted agreement.

Groot kept his eyes on the rumbling cart. "What about Bapu? What if he gets the elephant?"

Babcock pulled a knife from his belt. "Then we've got ourselves an elephant as well as a donkey cart."

The peasant's strange, high-pitched wail grew louder as the little black donkey clip-clopped past the ditch.

The three men wrinkled their noses as the cart

passed them, a strong odour wafting from its wooden boards.

Babcock muttered, "Cow shit."

Groot whispered, "Dung cakes. Indian burn dung cakes for fuel."

Rising to his knees, Babcock motioned Mustafa and Groot to follow. "You two take Grandpa. I'll grab the animal."

Mustafa drew a leather garrotte from his pocket, his fists clenching both ends of the thin weapon.

As the three men crept from the ditch, a short distance down the road the cart slowed and the peasant turned in the seat. Lowering the mantle from his head, he raised the fingers of his right hand, making an obscene gesture at the men.

Babcock bolted upright from his crouch. "Bapu!"

Groot and Mustafa stopped and stood upright.

Laughing, Bapu snapped the reins as Land Group ran down the dusty track after the rattling donkey cart.

21

A Tamil Trader

SEA GROUP

A full moon reflected silver across a western pocket of
the Bay of Bengal as Adam Horne sat alongside Jud
on the narrow bench of the *masulah* which Sea Group
had taken from the coastal village of Attur. Jingee and
Kiro lay on hemp bags of rice, lentils and betel leaves
stowed aboard the thin-shelled vessel. Its four oars
were turned inward from the hull. Horne held the arm
of the teakwood rudder. Jud gripped the bowline attached to the lateen sail. The night's wind filled the
triangular canvas, carrying Sea Group northwards
along the Coromandel Coast, towards the anchorage
called the Madras Roads.

Sea Group had been lucky in Attur. So far everything was going smoothly. Too smoothly. Would they
have to pay for this run of good luck? Horne felt easier

when good fortune was balanced by at least the threat of trouble.

Wearing a *dhoti* knotted around his groin like the other three men, with no shirt or shoes, Horne sat in the balmy night with one bare foot resting on the bench, reviewing the progress they had made since disembarking from the *Eclipse* early this morning.

The landing had been at precisely the right inlet. The hike to Attur, quick and easy. They had received a warm reception from the Ranga Pilar family who had given them the exact boat Horne had wanted. Now they were enjoying a strong coastal wind. Was Land Group faring this well?

Reviewing the plans he had synchronized for the two groups, Horne remembered that the mission was meant to benefit the East India Company in some way not revealed to him.

The wind caressed his cheek as he thought about the power and size of the Honourable East India Company: their headquarters was halfway around the world from this isolated spot; it was run by the Court of Directors, twenty-four men elected by a Court of Proprietors, merchants and bankers who owned the Company's so-called "stock."

Horne did not consider himself to be a businessman but he was intrigued by that revolutionary new commercial concept called "stock." It had been devised by the East India Company to raise money for voyages to the Orient, a plan in which they sold pieces of each voyage's profits to investors and called it "stock" in the voyage.

Would the idea of selling "stock" spread to other

trading companies? Would more companies become as large as the East India Company with tentacles reaching around the world? Would other companies also commission their own Marine? Mercenary armies? Would battles for power and world markets develop among those companies? Would wars break out as they did between nations?

Enjoying the night's breeze, Horne watched Jud holding the line to the triangular sail and wondered what he was thinking. Jud had told him how he had lost his wife in childbirth and how desolation had driven him to a bad life, the reason he had ended up in prison. What did the East India Company mean to Jud? Did he think of it as anything more than a strange group of faceless white men who owned ships, built gaols, traded for spices and silks and tea? Would Jud profit from serving the Company? Being a Bombay Marine?

Looking at Jingee and Kiro curled peacefully on the hemp bags, he thought that, yes, his seven men from the Bombay prisons had already benefited from the Company and this mysterious mission. They had been freed from gaol, exonerated.

He had, however, warned all the men about the possibility of being caught and tried for treason. Feeling the Bay's gentle current tremble the rudder in his hand, he smiled as he remembered Babcock's simple, straightforward answer.

"We were in prison when you found us. You're the only one with something to lose." Babcock had added, smiling, "So us prison rats have got to watch over you."

Horne had not previously considered that he was the only man of the squadron who had not been in prison, and remembering how Babcock had teased him that they would protect him, Horne wondered if he had not only found seven new Marines but also seven new friends. He recalled his doubts about forming any kind of personal attachments to people. Had he been wrong?

Jingee lay on the hemp bags unable to sleep, still too excited by the reception his relations in Attur had given him and the three foreigners whom they had called *topiwallahs*—men who wore hats.

The moment Jingee had stepped across the threshold of his cousins' home in Attur, he had felt as if he had come back to India after a long journey to a distant land, or that his three years in the prison of Bombay Castle had been some awful dream where there had been no sunlight, no jasmine, no saffron, no brilliant colours like yellow and green and pink—all small but important parts of the world to him.

Little had changed in the village of Attur—nor in the Ranga Pilar house—since Jingee had last been there four years ago. The village's maze of white plastered walls. Bushes draped with laundry drying in the sun. The palmyra doors opening to the family's court-yard. A garden of mango and lemon and tamarind trees. The smell of incense lingering in the salons cur-tained with blue-and-white striped cotton to block the midday sun.

The Pilar family's fortune had been secured more than a hundred years ago, during the days of the Dutch control of Porto Novo on the Coromandel Coast. The great-great-great grandfather and founder of the clan, Ananda Rangai Pilar, had been the *dubash* to Holland's factor in India. Since that time the family had prospered and spread to adjoining towns and villages, their interests including fishing, brass works, pottery, but always as before—acting as agents for wealthy *topiwallahs*.

A cousin to Ranga Pilar, Jingee had been warmly welcomed by the men of the family. The women kept a proper distance, sprinkling the ground with rose water, spreading blankets, producing an array of food as brightly coloured as their billowing silk *saris*: spiced lamb nestling in a bed of yellow rice, layers of pastry and lamb, a delicate *masala* cooked in a clay oven and tasting of turmeric, mint, ginger, an explosion of flavours which had reminded Jingee how much he had to learn about cooking if he was to serve Captain Horne a truly fine meal.

As Jingee lay on the hemp bags under the stars twinkling over the Bay of Bengal, he remembered how Horne's request for a surf boat had been received with mirth by his cousins. But when the Pilar brothers had seen that the *topiwallahs* were serious, they had taken them to a beach shed, letting Horne have his choice of boats. They had next escorted him to a circle of native fishermen sitting cross-legged in a circle mending nets. The old men had explained how to row a rope-sewn boat through the three stages of the tricky Madras surf.

Horne's voice jolted Jingee's reminiscences. Sitting up on the bags, he saw the Captain pointing out into the night's darkness.

Kiro, awakened by Horne's voice, sat alert next to

Jingee. They both saw the dark outline of the ship to the east.

Horne lashed the rudder to its coir line, moving aft to the hemp bags lined along the hull.

As Horne began moving bags to make a place to conceal himself, Jud and Kiro took their places by two oars. Jingee pushed the last bags behind Horne, draping fishnet over them, and hurried to pull a robe over his *dhoti*.

"Ahoy! Ahoy there!" Jingee swung a lantern back and forth in an arc. "Ahoy!"

High above the *masulah* in the night, a voice answered from the frigate, a reply spoken in English and magnified by a speaking trumpet. "What pass do you show?"

Jingee kept waving the lantern. "I come from the village of Attur."

Jud and Kiro stood at the two oars, their eyes cast down to the hemp bags in front of them, both posing as servants to a Tamil trader. When the waves bumped the *masulah* against the English ship, Kiro extended his oar, preventing repeated impacts from damaging the surf boat's thin shell, but never raising his eyes to the ship.

An officer in a notched hat appeared in the light of the frigate's port entry, the gold braid on his uniform glittering in the lantern's glow; two seamen dropped a rope ladder to the *masulah*, and the officer began the descent, followed by two of the ship's Marines wearing red jackets, tall shako hats, their muskets fixed with steel bayonets.

Jingee welcomed the officer with a deep, ostentatious salaam. Accepting the greeting with a curt nod, the fair-skinned Second Lieutenant directed the Marines to opposite sides of the bobbing boat as he held out one hand—palm upward—to Jingee, demanding, "Your pass."

"I need no pass. I am Ragi Pilar, merchant from Attur." Jingee looked haughtily from the Lieutenant to the Marines, one of whom was moving towards Jud while the other was stepping over bags to where Horne was hidden in the stern.

"Haven't you heard in Attur, Mr. Pilar, that there's a war being fought?"

Jingee insisted, "I am only a trader, sahib."

The Lieutenant glanced at Kiro and Jud. "These two are your men?"

Jingee dismissed them with a wave of the hand. "Sickly and eat too much, both of the *feringhi* dogs."

"Why are you travelling at night?"

"My father is an old man, sahib. I sat with him in the garden until sunset. Then I hurried to leave because I must reach Madras before dawn. I have a stall in the Bazaar."

"Attur? That's the village down the coast."

Hearing bayonets slicing the hemp bags, the sound of rice and lentils spilling onto deck, Jingee shrieked, "Sahib, stop your men! They're ruining my cargo!"

Ignoring Jingee's plea, the Lieutenant asked, "Did you see any ships on your trip north from Attur? French ships at any point along the coast?"

Jingee's attention was divided between the mention of French ships and the two British Marines stabbing bayonets into bags, approaching the spot where Horne was hidden under the fishnet.

Wringing his hands, Jingee pleaded, "Lieutenant, your men have made enough damage. Please stop them."

"You have no trading permit?"

"My stall is in the Black Town, sahib. I require no document to sell to my people."

Looking from Jingee to the ripped bags spilling provisions across the boat, the Lieutenant called wearily, "Bullitt, back aboard ship. Kettlestone, there's nothing here."

The Marine, Kettlestone, moved towards the ladder, but the other man, Bullitt, kept stabbing, driving his bayonet into the bags, one hand pushing down on the musket's butt.

"Let's *go*, Bullitt!"

Jingee watched the three men finally climb overhead into darkness, waiting until the rope ladder was pulled up behind them.

Jud and Kiro put their strength into the oars, moving the *masulah* quickly away from the frigate as Jingee fell to his knees in the stern, digging frantically amongst the torn hemp and scattered foodstuffs. "Captain sahib! Captain sahib! Are you hurt?"

The boat listed. Jingee turned. He saw a figure raising itself from the Bay, muscled arms pulling the dripping body into the boat.

"Captain sahib!"

Gulping for air, Horne fell across the ripped bags. "What'd they say about French . . . ships?"

"You heard, Captain sahib?"

Horne nodded, still gulping for air after holding his breath beneath water. "I heard . . . just as I was going under the . . . fishnets."

22

The Untouchables

LAND GROUP

The black donkey clip-clopped along the narrow road winding through the Chingleput Hills, the sky dark and twinkling with stars, the scattered settlements looking more prosperous the closer Land Group moved to Fort St. George.

Bapu held the leather reins loose in his hands; Groot sat beside him, his blue cap pushed back on his sun-bleached blond hair as he asked questions about India. Babcock and Mustafa slept in the bed of the bumping wagon, unbothered by the two men's voices, the cart's jerky movements, or the lingering smell of dung cakes.

"Who's the ruler of India?"

"The Grand Mughul. He holds court in the Diwani-i-am in the city of Agra."

"Does the Mughul have a parliament or council that makes the laws?"

"The Mughul's word is the one law of India. That is why Tamils here in the South do not like the Mughul. They've remained faithful to the old Hindu religion while many Northerners have taken the Muslim ways of the Mughul. India is a country of different religions. The Hindus. The Muslims. A third religion here is the Sikhs. Now you Europeans are bringing us a fourth. Christianity."

Remembering how Bapu had been slow in the learning sessions with Horne, Groot was surprised to hear how clearly, how intelligently the bandit leader spoke about his country. Bapu had explained that a district sheriff in Rajasthan had taught him to speak English.

Groot said, "I understand that India is divided by castes. How many castes are there?"

"Four."

"Which caste are you?"

"By birth, I am a *Kshatriya*, the second highest caste. I am descended from the line of warriors called the Rajput. But I do not fool myself. I have no rights, no privileges, no powers of my caste. I live no better than a *Sudra*. The *Sudras* are the fourth, the lowest caste. The third is the *Vaisya*, the caste of traders and merchants. I think Horne's man, Jingee, is a *Vaisya*. There are also the people called the *Panchamas*. That means the 'fifth.' The *Panchamas* include people who fall outside the four castes. They are also called the Untouchables."

"Untouchables?"

Bapu nodded, his swarthy face looking peaceful as he huddled over the donkey, his closely-spaced eyes held on the road. "People will not touch the *Pancha-mas* for fear of becoming polluted."

"Polluted by what?"

"Bad spirits. There are also lowly people called the Unseeables. They carry bells to warn members of the high castes to look away when they are approaching them. But the lowest people in India are called the *Chensu Carir*. They are so offensive that they are condemned to roam the country, carrying their few belongings tied to the backs of scrawny donkeys. They are not allowed to stop at any one spot and make a home. You will see them alongside the road, picking ants from the earth to feed to their children."

Groot thought of Amsterdam, the healthy, red-cheeked children there, cheery women with broad hips and scarves tied under their chubby chins, the old men sitting around wooden tables covered with bright carpets and drinking tall glasses of golden beer. Groot had no family left alive but he nevertheless felt homesick, faraway from that cosy world of red brick houses and windows criss-crossed with lace panels, of pigs turning on a spit over a crackling fire and swing-kettles bubbling with chicken stews.

The India which Groot knew seemed barren in contrast to Holland, and he asked, "How can people go on living so miserably here?"

"Hindus believe that after death we shall be reborn to a higher caste if we have lived a good life, perhaps even coming back to earth as one of the highest order, the *Brahmins*, the priests who own the fields and control all the produce. Some men say that they were the first people to come to India. They say that the *Brah-*

mins took all the land and made a system to protect themselves from losing it. It is only in recent years that Europeans have come to India and given that system a name. The Portuguese who came here gave us their word *castas*—caste."

"Muslims and *Brahmins* and Portuguese. Bapu, India seems to me to be a land that's always being conquered."

Bapu shrugged. "Perhaps that's our *dharma*."

"What's *dharma*?"

"No Europeans can understand the meaning of *dharma*. We believe it tells us who we are, how to be true to the caste to which we have been born. Battle is the *dharma* of the *Kshatriya* caste. I am born to fight. I was true to my caste before I was imprisoned at Bombay Castle. But prison is against my *dharma*."

"Was it part of your caste or your *dharma* to rob and steal when you were a bandit?"

"My glory is to fight. My honour is battle. I think Horne has the same *dharma*. He is a warrior. He would make a good Indian Rajput if he did not ignore the world inside him." Bapu touched his chest. "We Indians respect the world inside us. More than the world around us." He motioned to the night, then paused, his hand hovering in mid-air as he spotted a light in the distance.

Groot looked in the direction where Bapu was staring. He saw the dim glow of a flickering bonfire beside the road. He hopped from the cart as Bapu drew on the reins.

Behind them, Babcock bolted up from his sleep. "Why'd we stop?"

"Shhh." Bapu raised his hand. "There's a blockade ahead."

"Blockade? What kind? English?"

"Groot's gone to see."

Mustafa raised himself from the bed, rubbing his eyes, turning his head to see why they had stopped.

Babcock knelt beside Bapu, trying to count the men grouped around the fire. There were at least a dozen soldiers.

Groot returned from his quick reconnoitre, his blue cap pushed back on his prickly blond hair, his pale eyes wide with excitement as he whispered, "French!"

The four men hurried to unknot their canvas pack and began making the necessary preparations.

Groot, the only man of Sea Group who spoke French, drove the cart as Bapu huddled on the bench beside him, a turban wrapped around his bristly hair, the soiled mantle draped over his shoulders. Babcock and Mustafa lay in the back of the cart, water splashed on their bodies from the skin bag to look like splotches of feverish perspiration. All four men wore oddments of French military equipment—blue jacket, yellow sash, brown cap, brass-studded cross-belts, insignia.

Groot reined the donkey as three men moved from the darkness, the dancing flames glittering on their dusty blue-and-yellow uniforms.

Babcock began moaning as the wagon slowed, elbowing Mustafa to follow his example.

One Frenchman moved to speak to Groot while the other two soldiers leaned over the back of the cart.

They quickly recoiled at the smell from the bed and the sight of the fever-soaked bodies.

Grabbing one of the men's arms, Babcock licked his lips, mumbling feverish gibberish. The Frenchman jerked free from the American's clutch, both men holding their noses against the stench as they moved back towards the guard questioning Groot.

The three Frenchmen huddled together near the front of the cart, speaking in low whispers. They beckoned two more men from the fire. The conference continued, the men glancing towards the cart as they spoke.

The first guard stepped back to the wagon, snapped a few words to Groot and stood back, waving his hand and ordering, *"Allez! Allez!"*

Groot mumbled to Bapu.

Springing angrily to his feet, Bapu shouted to the French soldiers in the Urdu dialect of the Sepoy camps. The Frenchman kept waving his hand, shouting for the wagon to pass. Bapu jabbed a forefinger at Babcock and Mustafa in the back of the cart, still shrieking in Urdu at the Frenchmen. But Groot snapped the reins and the little donkey slowly clattered down the road. As the cart passed the French soldiers by the fire, they turned away their heads, holding their hands to their noses against the smell.

When the fire's red glow finally receded in the darkness, Babcock lifted himself from the bed, whispering, "What happened?"

Groot kept his eyes on the rocky road. "I told them no village or camp would give us shelter. That you two have—How you say it? Yellow Fever?"

"And?"

"I asked them if we could sleep by their fire."

"And?"

"No. They refused."

"They sent us away?"

"Yah, they say they have no medicine. That it's better if we keep going."

"Go where?"

"They didn't say. Just go, go. *Allez, allez.*"

"The bastards."

Bapu looked over his shoulder at Babcock. "What are you complaining about, man? We got through, yes?"

"But what if we really *were* dying?"

Bapu frowned. "You might be dying if you go on talking so loudly."

Mustafa grunted, his dark eyes surveying the far shadows.

23

The Madras Roads

SEA GROUP

Adam Horne sailed as far north as he dared go in the *masulah*, travelling until Sea Group came within sight of merchant ships in their anchorage, near enough to see the masts, spars, and rigs tilting in the turbulent surf, the roar of the Madras Roads sounding like a river crashing over rapids.

From the cluster of ships tossing at anchor, Horne and his men looked across the churning white water towards the walls of Fort St. George. Turrets rose at both ends of the castellated walls. Ramparts slanted down to the waves crashing onto the white beach. Rows of cannon were trained towards the sea.

The spectacle reminded Jud of Sheik Al Hadd's Castle of the Golden Sand stretching along the coast of Oman. He thought of Maringa's death, he remembered the promise he had made to the spirit of his dead son the night Horne had rescued him from the maintop mast aboard the *Eclipse* and how, in turn, he himself had saved Horne's life. Looking at the yellow walls of Fort St. George, he made another quick prayer to the spirit of his son, thanking the dead boy for helping them to get this far. From here onward he knew they would have to use human powers.

Kiro also was reminded of scenes from his past. He had stood as a child in the pine forest above the Suonada and, looking at the Dawn Palace, had thought how he would storm it with a team of *Ninja* raiders when he reached manhood. Adam Horne had helped him come closer to that dream than he had ever been. Having chosen him from prison, Horne had helped Kiro prove to himself he could be as elite as a *Ninja*. The time had come to show his worthiness.

Jingee stood beside Horne in the *masulah*, looking across the crashing surf at Fort St. George, wondering what awaited them beyond this point? Would Horne keep him in the squadron? Where would they go from here? Would he be able to go on serving Horne? He hoped so. Horne raised service to an honour.

Hurrying Sea Group to dismantle the *masulah*'s mast and rudder, Horne stowed them with the sails to prevent them from injuring someone in a capsize. Having dumped the hemp bags of foodstuffs overboard, the four men began folding their equipment—uniforms, boots, Chinese explosives, knives, everything they would use later—into compact leather packets which they secured to their belts.

Wearing nothing except *dhotis* and leather belts dangling with the waterproof packets, the four men waited

at the oars as the current began speeding them towards
the surf.

"Row!" Horne shouted as the surf grabbed the boat,
and the men began moving their oars in unison. The
wave tilted them. Tipped them. Twisted the *masulah*'s
pliable hull. The boat was pitched upwards. Dashed
forwards. Dropped into a trough with a thud. Skittering
along what seemed to be a surface of smooth glass, the
boat flew to the peak of the next breaker as a wave
rose behind it, chasing it, dropping it, flooding it with
the wash. A brief pause followed the deluge—the few
seconds of the surf's middle stage—before the next
wave roared behind the boat, sweeping it to a new
crest. Feeling as if they were being dropped in mid-
air, the men were pummelled by another wave, and the
boat began to recede, carried back out to sea with the
wash of the tide. For this, the third and most dangerous
stage of the surf, Horne began shouting, *"Forward . . .
forward . . . forward . . ."* and the men plied their oars
against the backwash of the tide, rowing to the time of
the shouts as the hull twisted and strained from the
force. Another breaker rose beneath them. A crack
filled the air. The boat was hurled upwards. It flipped,
emptying, Horne, Jingee, Kiro and Jud into the thundering white surf.

"Guard!" Thomas Lally beat the arm of his wooden
crucifix on the door of his prison. "You'll get no sleep,
Guard, till you move me from this room! I demand to
be moved, Guard!"

During the night, Lally had realised that the French

would try to assassinate him. He was certain of it. They
would know by now that he had surrendered Pondicherry. They would suspect him of trying to trade military secrets with the British for his life. They would
show no mercy. His mother had been French. King
Louis had made him Baron de Tolendahl. He was a
hero in France. But his father had been Irish and—to
the French in times of defeat—he would be no different from a full-blooded Briton. An assassin was probably on the way to silence him at this very moment.

Gripping the crucifix in his hand, Lally chopped it
against the door, shouting, "Guard! I demand to be
moved to a safer prison, Guard! *Guard! I demand to
be moved! MOVED!*"

24
Fort St. George

THE BLACK TOWN

Like the hours of daytime, Indian nights were divided
into four *pahars*. It was the time of the fourth *pahar*—
shortly before dawn—when the woman named Prasada
was working by lamplight in the garden room of the
dancing-girl house she kept on Adams Street in the
jumble of wooden and clay houses beyond the North
Wall of Fort St. George—the native section of Madras
called the Black Town.

Prasada, a small-boned Indian woman in her late
thirties, wore turquoise silk trousers with a matching
overskirt, and a yellow mantle edged with glittering
gold bangles. A delicate golden ring pierced her left
nostril and small ornamental bells jangled from the fil-
igree bracelets encircling her wrists and ankles. Her
eyes were painted with antimony and kohl, and a blue

tilaka spot was centred between her thinly pencilled eyebrows.

Sitting cross-legged on a Persian carpet, Prasada counted piles of coins in front of her on the floor. She jotted numbers onto small slips of paper, rolled each paper, stuck them into bamboo tubes, and dropped the tubes into a reed basket. This was her system of accounts.

Dancing girls. Dice. The *hookah*: Rice beer. Spiced beer. Arrack. Glasses of hemp called *bhang*. Plates of rolled betel leaves. Bowls of opium balls. Prasada provided whatever her customers required but prided herself that she employed no *Nautch* girls—common whores.

Prasada's business could have been better if her house had adjoined the taverns and punch-houses on Main Gate Street, the thoroughfare leading to Fort St. George. The Black Town obeyed Hindu rules, however, and as a woman of the Dancing Girl caste was not allowed to live on the same street as a *Brahmin*, Prasada could not run her establishment near the priests' house.

Hurrying to finish her accounts so that she could go to sleep before sunrise, Prasada paused when she heard shouting in the night.

Sitting motionless, trying not to jangle her bells and bracelets, she wondered who could be making so much noise at this hour. Trouble-makers? Thieves?

The sound of running feet moved across the courtyard and, stopping outside the amber beads hanging from the arched entrance, an excited voice called, "Lady Prasada! Lady Prasada!"

Prasada recognized the voice and frowned. "Shashi, what do you want?"

A slim Indian male servant clattered through the beaded curtain, falling face down in front of Prasada, his turban pressed to the carpet, his arms stretching in front of him, the white twists of his *dhoti* protruding into the air like tail feathers.

"Shashi, what is the meaning of this?"

"Thieves, Lady Prasada! Thieves came and took her!"

"Took *whom*, Shashi?"

"Jasmine, Lady Prasada! Thieves came and took Jasmine!"

"How many strangers, Shashi?"

"Four, Lady Prasada. One was a big man with eyes close together like a snake. I think the others were English, Lady Prasada."

Shashi explained how four men had awakened him from his sleep in the stables and had held a knife to his throat. They had tied a rope around the neck of the four-ton cow elephant named Jasmine and led her from the stables.

Prasada considered the situation. If she sent Shashi after the thieves, the lazy devil might sneak off and go to sleep. If she pursued the villains herself, she would have to call upon the Fort Guards, and that might involve an official search of her house. She did not want that.

Deciding on the safest action, she reached into the basket of bamboo tubes. "Captain Green can pay for Jasmine."

Astonished, Shashi sat back on his haunches. "But

Captain Green didn't take Jasmine, Lady Prasada. It was strangers! *Feringhi!*"

"I know. I know. But Jasmine's gone and somebody's got to pay for her." She clattered through the bamboo tubes in the basket.

Kneeling in front of Prasada, Shashi continued, "Oh, the four strangers smelled so bad." He held his snub brown nose between his thumb and forefinger.

Prasada ignored him as she dug for the English Captain's account.

"Before the strangers took Jasmine, Lady Prasada, they climbed into her water barrel. It was very, very funny to see Jasmine put her trunk into the barrel and gave them a bath!"

Holding his stomach, Shashi laughed at the picture of the elephant spraying water onto the naked strangers. "Oh, Lady Prasada! Jasmine's such a *Nautch* girl!"

Prasada waved her hand irritably. "Forget about Jasmine. She ate too much anyway. I am thankful she's gone. Now tell me how much rope they took so I can—"

She raised her eyes in time to see Shashi reaching into a blue-and-white bowl standing next to the carpet.

"Thief!" Prasada hurled the bamboo tube at her servant. "Dirty little *Sudra* thief!"

Rolling backwards, Shashi clattered through the hanging beads, laughing as he ran across the courtyard, one fist clutched to his chest.

Cursing to herself, Prasada added five opium balls to Captain Green's account. She knew that the English officer would pay any amount to keep his wife from learning he visited a dancing-girl's house. Without jealous English wives, Prasada could not have made a living in the Black Town.

THE MAIN GATE

Land Group, bathed and changed into clothing they had carried in canvas packs from the *Eclipse*, walked with an elephant along Main Gate Street through the Black Town. The time was still in the fourth *pahar*—shortly before dawn.

Adjoining the North Wall of Fort St. George, the buildings of the Black Town were as varied as its inhabitants: Hindu pagodas rubbed shoulders with columned English façades; a jumble of brown clay hovels crowded next to the stately wooden home of a Portuguese merchant; brightly painted swing-signs hung in front of 'The London Tavern' and 'The Mayfair Coffee House.' There were Armenian cookshops, Persian astrologers, Arabian chandlers.

Babcock, dressed in twill breeches, shirt, and brown boots, his hands clasped behind his back, idly wagged a leather riding crop as he ambled towards two round streetlamps glowing on either side of the open fortress gates ahead of him.

Groot and Mustafa followed him down Main Gate Street, also dressed in the twill clothing worn by clerks working for the East India Company in Madras. Walking with their arms round each other's shoulders, they stumbled like two friends who had spent a long night in a tavern. Both were better actors than Babcock had expected. Horne would be proud of them.

Bapu, wearing a *dhoti* and a turban wrapped around

his head, and looking like a true Asian, lagged behind
the three men, leading the elephant and carrying a large
coil of rope in his other hand.

Waiting for the others to catch up with him, Babcock
idled by the Bazaar intersecting Main Gate Street less
than a hundred feet from the fortress's North Wall.
Farmers were still unloading fruit and vegetables from
their buffalo and donkey carts. Lights flickered in
hanging jars festooned from stalls opened for early
morning trade.

Turning back toward the Main Gate, Babcock ca-
sually approached a gatehouse to the right of the gates
where two guards sat inside playing dice.

Leaning his head into the small kiosk, Babcock
asked, "Who gets the gifts?"

The shorter guard looked blankly at Babcock.
"Gifts?"

Babcock thumbed over his shoulder. "There's an elephant out here for Governor Pigot. A gift from some
rajah in Bangalore. The papers for it are arriving today.
But the *mahoot*'s got to do something with the animal
'tween now and then."

Outside the guardhouse, Bapu stood smiling in front
of the elephant, wagging his turban from side to side.

The guard lowered his eyes to the pair of three-sided
dice. "Show him where the Stables are."

Babcock stepped farther into the gatehouse, lowering his voice. "Can't you take care of this, jack? My
mates and me, we had a long night—"

Outside the gatehouse, Groot and Mustafa began
wailing at the streetlamp, like wolves howling at a new
moon.

The guard picked up the leather dice cup. "Take your friends and get lost."

Babcock hiccuped. "Come on, jack—"

"I said, get lost."

Babcock shrugged. "If you say so, jack—"

Turning from the kiosk, Babcock called to Groot and Mustafa, "Come on, mates. Let's give this man here a hand."

Bapu surrendered the thick coil of rope to Mustafa and, gripping the elephant's lead, he and Mustafa walked through the open gates of Fort St. George, followed by Babcock and Groot.

THE KING'S BARRACKS

Main Gate Street was cobbled inside the fortress walls. The houses lining both sides of the street were freshly whitewashed and uniformly decorated with green shutters. A straight line of coconut-oil streetlamps ran down the right side of the street, glowing like a row of luminescent dandelion balls in the early morning darkness.

Babcock and Groot followed the elephant down Main Gate Street. Stepping to one side of the elephant, Babcock took a look at the inner fortress at the end of the street, then resumed his place beside Groot. "Straight ahead of us are the walls of the Governor's House."

Groot raised his eyes to the right, seeing a church spire rising above the neat row of two-storey buildings. "There's the Portuguese Church."

The air seemed fresher inside the fortress, less

tainted by the stench of burning manure cakes, the sickly smell of rotting fruit and garbage heaped in gutters which had pervaded the Black Town.

Bapu and Mustafa turned right at the end of Main Gate Street, leading the elephant into a wide cobbled stretch, moving towards a row of yellow stone buildings facing another wide expanse of cobblestone.

Babcock and Groot followed the slowly plodding elephant, alert for landmarks and buildings they had studied with Horne in the shipboard session.

Knowing they were crossing Portuguese Square, Babcock looked left and saw an iron grille embedded into the wall of the Governor's House. He guessed that it must be the gate to the Magazine, the fort's store of ammunition and explosives. Smiling, he felt the leather pouch hanging from his belt.

Approaching the top end of Portuguese Square, Bapu and Mustafa turned left, leading the elephant across the cobbled avenue towards the Stables.

Babcock and Groot remained standing at the top of Portuguese Square, acquainting themselves with the fort's layout.

Swinging the riding crop behind him, Babcock said, "This wide stretch here is called the Parade. The Stables and Storehouses are down to our left. The King's Barracks to our right. There in front of us is the Guardhouse."

Groot, who was studying the Guardhouse, elbowed Babcock. "Look."

Babcock studied the three-storey building standing directly in front of them, with bales of straw piled along the façade, and raised his eyes to the deep stone porches on each floor above the iron entry gate.

Groot elbowed him again. "The gate! Look inside the gate!"

Babcock saw what Groot meant. Two men were unlocking the gate. From the inside.

"Relax, man." Babcock raised his eyes up the front of the narrow building, remembering how the upper floors were divided into T's, hallways leading to long rear corridors.

Groot watched the men inside the gate. "What are they doing there? It's not light yet."

"It's better they're doing it now than when Horne gets there, whatever it is." Babcock turned to his right. "Let's go."

Walking in the opposite direction from Bapu and Mustafa, Babcock led Groot towards the King's Barracks standing at the north side of the Parade. Approaching a small window lit from within by a flickering yellow light, Babcock rapped the butt of his riding crop on a pane of wavy glass.

The window opened. A craggy-faced officer wearing the tan-and-red uniform of His Majesty's 64th Regiment stuck out his head.

Babcock knew there was little friendship between Company employees and the Military stationed inside Fort St. George. He was appropriately brusque. "I want to see Fenner."

"*Captain* Fenner?"

Babcock nodded. "I want to speak to him about a gift for *Governor* Pigot."

"What kind of gift?"

"Who takes custody, Captains or Lieutenants?"

The Lieutenant repeated more testily. "What kind of gift?"

Babcock stepped closer to the window. "A bloody big elephant, that's what. I know Fenner's in charge of the Stables. I also know he sleeps here in this lice-infested barracks. So I'm—"

The clatter of marching boots began echoing from across the cobbled Parade.

Turning, Babcock and Groot saw eight uniformed men marching out of the Guardhouse, an armed squadron escorting a man from the iron gate of the Guardhouse, a white-haired man clutching a crucifix to his chest.

The Barracks Lieutenant poked his head farther out of the window. "What the hell—"

Pulling back inside, he shouted behind him, "Kyle, where are they taking Lally?"

Babcock and Groot exchanged glances. They looked back to the guards marching Lally across the Parade towards the top of Portuguese Square.

The Lieutenant shouted louder inside the house. "Lally's being moved from the Guardhouse, Kyle! Get your arse out here!"

Stepping away from the window, Babcock whispered to Groot, "Follow Lally. See where they're taking him."

Groot's blue eyes were round with excitement. "Where do you go?"

"To tell Horne about this change."

"Where are you going to see the *schupper*?"

"Stop worrying, Groot. You just find out where they're moving Lally. Meet me—" Babcock thought of a good place for a rendezvous. "Meet me below Portuguese Square. At the foot of the Governor's House. The south end. Do you remember where that is?"

"Yah." Nodding, Groot spoke as if he were reciting for Horne aboard the *Eclipse*. "The south side of the Governor's House is also called St. Thomas Street. St. Thomas Street runs north to south, leading to St. Thomas Gate on the south—"

"Good man." Babcock thrust the riding crop towards his chest. "Here. Take this with you."

Groot stared quizzically at the riding crop. "Why this?"

"So you look important."

Babcock turned and took long strides across the cobbled Parade, the leather pouch slapping against the side of his breeches.

THE NABOB'S BASTION

At the opposite end of the Parade from the King's Barracks, Mustafa and Bapu led the elephant into the Stables. Bapu called loudly in Hindi for hay and water for the animal, creating a commotion for the *mahoot* on night duty as Mustafa moved quickly towards the back wall, finding the door to the steps which led up to the West Wall.

The inner stairwell was narrow, rising steeply, and the sound of Bapu's orders grew fainter as Mustafa felt his way in the darkness lit only by shafts of dark morning light pouring through apertures gashed into the stonework.

Carrying the coil of rope in one hand, he halted at the top of the stone steps in front of an iron-banded door. Listening, he pulled back the bolt and—slowly— pushed open the door.

Stepping outside onto a narrow walkway, he flattened himself against the wall, looking cautiously to his left and then to his right. All was clear and, pulling a slice of cork from his shirt pocket, he shut the door and bent to plug the cork at its base. Then he grabbed the rope and began edging his way to the left, moving towards the low-tiled roof of Nabob's Bastion, a circular structure on pillars, silhouetted like a mushroom against the inky blue sky.

A guard stood by one of the pillars, a lone figure leaning against his musket, looking eastwards towards the sky beginning to blot with the morning light, the surf crashing below him.

Mustafa began feeding rope from the coil of his other hand, moving closer towards the guard, and as he reached the corner of the West Wall, he looked down the length of the South Wall. He saw no one approaching from the far lookout—St. Thomas Bastion—and he made the last few steps.

The rope whistled over the guard's head. Mustafa tightened his grip until he felt the man weaken, the musket clattering to the stone floor.

Lowering the unconscious body, Mustafa stuffed a rag into the guard's mouth and corded it tightly with a leather thong. Binding the man's hands and feet, he rolled him past a pyramid of cannonballs.

Working quickly, he anchored one end of the rope to the base of a cannon and tossed the other end over the wall. He sat down beside the stack of cannonballs, aware that his heart was pounding. He was excited. He felt alive for the first time in—how long?

He realized he had not been this excited—this happy—in the eight years since he had left his parents' home in Alanya, after strangling his brother in a fight. Running away to the Turkish port of Izmir, he had joined the Ottoman Navy and served aboard one of the Sultan's warships until he was recognized by a man who remembered him from Alanya. He had jumped ship in Port Said and joined a merchant crew of the East India Company in Suez.

After fighting with and fatally garrotting a Greek sailor aboard the Company merchant ship, Mustafa was condemned to Bombay Castle.

He had thought he was going to be imprisoned in the dungeons there for the rest of his life and had been immediately suspicious when Adam Horne had chosen him from the other criminals to go to Bull Island. At first he had feared that he was being sent back to Turkey, then that he was being taken to a life of hard labour in a penal colony. But Horne had been telling the truth. Mustafa had not been imprisoned. He had been fed, exercised, trained and brought on a mission as Horne had promised.

But Mustafa was still confused. This was not work. This was not war. Horne had even cautioned them to try to avoid taking men's lives! So what kind of navy—or army—was this "Bombay Marine"? What kind of officer didn't want you to kill men?

Sitting beside the unconscious guard in the Nabob's Bastion, Mustafa remembered how Land Group had entered the fortress, how they had passed so easily in front of the guard's very eyes, and he began to laugh.

He was still laughing when the rope tugged against his leg.

He laughed louder. Look! He had caught himself a fish!

Oh, yes, he liked being a Bombay Marine. What would their next mission be?

25

Old Acquaintances

THE GUARDHOUSE

Sea Group reached the base of the fortress's South Wall and Adam Horne immediately found the rope dangling from the Nabob's Bastion. After testing that it was securely attached across the overhead battlements, he stepped back for Kiro to lead the climb up the wall.

Dressed in twill breeches, shirt and tall boots, like the rest of Sea Group, Kiro moved quickly up the rope, a leather packet of explosives dangling from his belt as his hands gripped their way upwards, his feet walking the wall.

When he disappeared over the red tiled battlements, Jud followed, ascending as easily as he had scaled the shrouds and ratlines of the *Eclipse*. Jingee went next, gripping the rope, his turbanned head back, his dark eyes trained on the overhead goal, a leather packet of supplies dangling from the side of his breeches.

The leather wrappings had kept Sea Group's disguises and supplies dry when the *masulah* had capsized in the surf. No serious harm had been done except that the mishap had cost time, the surf washing them ashore a hundred yards farther down from the fortress's South Wall than Horne had wanted. A bamboo break had provided necessary cover for them to slip into the Company twill clothing and make a dash across the shipyards towards the South Wall.

Horne waited for Jingee to disappear into the Nabob's Bastion, then he too gripped the rope, moving upwards hand-over-hand, hoping there was enough darkness to cover his climb. Dawn would soon be breaking.

Swinging over the stone battlement, he saw that everyone—Mustafa included—had left for their posts. The only person remaining in the circular enclosure was the guard, bound and lying face down on the stone floor. The next change of watch would not be until six o'clock—the time when the bells rang in the English Church—and Horne hoped to be starting back to the Chingleput coastline by then.

Pulling up the rope from the wall, he took out his knife, slit off the length he needed, and dropped the rest over the bastion.

He glanced along the South Wall towards St. Thomas Bastion, but could see no one approaching on the watchwalk. Satisfied, he made his way down the West Wall with the small coil of rope, quickly finding the door flush with the stone. Falling to his knees, he pulled at the door's base and a piece of cork tumbled onto the stone step.

Closing the door behind him, he shot the bolt and waited until his eyes grew accustomed to the darkness. Then he descended the spiralling steps and swept one hand along the wall, halting when he felt the edges of a wooden hatch built into it. Locating its wire lock, he pushed open the hatch, threw out the rope and climbed out after it onto a flat roof.

He crawled on his stomach to the edge of the tiled roof and peered out at the fortress spread before him. The Governor's House stood in the centre, its walls thick and cornered by their own sturdy bastions. Beyond it rose the peaked roof of the Sea Gate, a row of columns leading from the gate to the entry of the Governor's House. The spire of the Portuguese Church rose to Horne's left, while to his right was the steeple of the English Church. The Parade ran directly below him; the King's Barracks to his left, the Stables to his right; he was on the roof of the Guardhouse.

Tightening one end of the rope to a stone kerb, Horne threw the other end over the front of the Guardhouse, wondering if Kiro had crossed the Parade by now and reached the English Church.

Looking southeast beyond the slim steeple of the English Church, he saw the arched roof of the side entrance, St. Thomas Gate. Jud and Jingee should be making their way there. Mustafa had a shorter distance to go, rejoining Bapu in the Stables to prepare the horses for escape, working to finish before the day shift came on duty.

A racket shattering the early morning's stillness answered Horne's question about Kiro's whereabouts.

At the sound of the pop, pop, popping of Chinese
fireworks exploding on the far side of the Governor's
House, he swung over the edge of the Guardhouse,
springing down the front wall and hoping that no glass
panes had been installed across the front of the porches
in the time since Governor Pigot had supplied Commodore Watson with details about the fortress.

Making his last spring, he swung beneath a sandstone cornice—and landed on stone floor!

Horne left the rope hanging down the front of the
Guardhouse, and flattened himself against a wall while
he took bearings in the darkness. There was no one in
the first hallway and, creeping along a stucco wall, he
moved to what he hoped was the back corridor.

Reaching the end of the wall, he listened before
peering around the corner.

The back corridor was long, lit by one torch sput-
tering in an iron wall-ring. Horne was surprised to see
no guard standing duty outside Lally's room. The place
seemed deserted.

Edging around the corner, he wondered if he had
entered the wrong building. Landed on the wrong floor.
Or had Lally's guard been changed earlier than usual
today? If so, where was the relief? Horne had planned
to create a diversion here with his own fireworks, a
ruse to give him the opportunity to tackle the guard.
But where was the guard?

He had now reached the door of what should be
Lally's prison. He stepped forward and saw that the
door was ajar.

Moving closer, he peered into the room.

Empty.

Slowly he pushed open the door and stepped into the whitewashed room, finding no window or torch-light there to give him light. Examining the room in the glow from the hall torch, he saw a narrow bed against one wall. He noticed that the mattress had been slept on. There was a table against the opposite wall with a candle and books. Reaching towards the table, he felt the candle's wax: it was still warm, pliable in his fingers. The titles of the books were French . . .

"*Stand where you are!*"

Horne spun around at the sound of the voice.

Two men blocked the doorway, the hall's torchlight glittering the gold epaulettes paired on their shoulders. The red coats, white breeches and gold stripes instantly identified them as officers in His Britannic Majesty's Army.

The taller of the two officers stepped into the room. He levelled a pistol at Horne. But, tilting his head to one side, he began to laugh, saying, "Why, I'll be damned. If it isn't . . . Adam Horne!"

A few stunned seconds passed before Horne recognized Oliver Giltspur.

Looking as rakish as Horne remembered him from London, Giltspur spoke in the same clipped manner which Horne also remembered—and loathed—from the days before he had come to India.

"Horne, what in damnation are you doing *here* of all places? I heard you'd joined the Bombay Marine." I say, that's the best outfit for you! The bloody Bombay—Buccaneers!"

"I'll take that as a compliment, Giltspur." Horne studied Giltspur's face, sideburns arched across high cheekbones, a thin aristocratic nose and strong chin.

"A compliment's not intended, Horne."

Turning to his companion, Giltspur explained, "Lieutenant, my old acquaintance here, Adam Horne, came out to this God-forsaken land of his own free will."

He turned back to Horne and asked, "Am I correct, Horne? Was it free choice? Or did you flee England after Starington killed Isabel . . . what was her name? Isabel *Springer*?"

Horne stepped forward. "I warn you, Giltspur. Don't say one word about Isabel."

Giltspur smirked, holding Horne's glare. "I remember why I never liked you, Horne. You were always too sure of yourself. Always so pleased with yourself and . . . Miss Springer!"

"Keep your mouth shut, Giltspur!"

Giltspur's laugh echoed in the bare room. "Horne, you are capital! Capital indeed! Here you are. Apprehended in a room occupied until recently by a valuable prisoner. And what do you do? *You* start giving *me* orders? What a rare fellow you are, Horne."

Horne appraised Giltspur and his companion, gauging how well both men were armed, how strongly they could block the door. He remembered there was no window behind him for escape.

Giltspur stepped farther into the room, one hand gripping the pistol. "What a capital position I'm in, Horne. Consider how many men would pay to change places with me at this moment. You do know, Horne, that men from the old days in London thought you were a sober, boring old stick. Who cared if you always won in those yard games? The model young gentleman who had so much to look forward to! Such a brilliant future! Do you know how many of the Mayfair set still despise you, Horne?"

"You are obviously one of them, Giltspur." Horne noticed that Giltspur's other hand rested on the hilt of his sabre.

"Tell me this, Horne. How exactly did your cherished Isabel get killed? I heard a story that Starington took her to Greeley's. Wasn't Greeley's the name of that stew in Bow Street which was the rage back in those days?"

"I warn you, Giltspur. Don't you say a word against Isabel—"

Giltspur laughed at Horne and went on. "The version I heard was that Starington told Isabel Greeley's was a private music club! He enticed her there by saying they would hear some new Purcell played by a quartet! Gad!" Throwing back his head, he laughed, "The only quartet at Greeley's would be four poxy wenches from Dublin!"

The Lieutenant joined in Giltspur's mirth, while Horne was rapidly forgetting about his duty.

"Of course, a fine young lady would not have heard about any place so vile as Greeley's," Giltspur continued. "But once inside she understood its purpose. As soon as they were ensconced in the front parlour, Starington tried to force himself on the delicious Isabel. He had drunk too much, and when your divine Isabel resisted his charms, he struck her a few times too many.

You arrived when Starington produced that pistol and fired. You bludgeoned him with a rather heavy object. A bit too heavy I'm told. The police came in a trice and old Ma Greeley hurriedly hid Starington's corpse. But there was nothing anybody could do with poor Isabel. She lay bleeding to death. Rather than allow her name be stained with scandal, you swore to the police that she and you had been set upon by toughs in the street and had taken refuge at Greeley's. Ma Greeley welcomed your gallant lie. Who wants the police shutting down a veritable gold mine?"

Horne was surprised that Giltspur had so much accurate information. He obviously thrived on the story.

Like men of his fast London set, Giltspur also enjoyed a good barb, and his voice thickened as he teased, "Come on, Horne. You were young and honorable back in those days and didn't talk much. But you're amongst gentlemen now. Officers of the King's Regiment. So share a story or two about how a tasty doxy like Isabel Springer felt when you got her alone, how easily she gave you her—"

Horne lunged for Giltspur.

As tall as Adam Horne, Captain Oliver Giltspur was also as solidly built. But Horne's attack surprised him, and he tumbled backwards onto the floor, the pistol clattering from his hand, the sabre tangling in his legs.

The other officer fell onto Horne's back, jerking to pull him from Giltspur. But Horne held on tightly, choking Giltspur's throat with one hand, pummelling his face with his fist.

Oblivious of Giltspur's blows, ignoring the Lieutenant's tugs on his back, his efforts to pull him away,

Horne fought against reason, not even noticing that another man had entered the room.

A voice shouted, "Don't go crazy, man! Don't go to pieces! Not here! Not now!"

Horne turned, gasping for breath, seeing Babcock standing beside him, a bloody knife in one hand.

Looking from Babcock to the Lieutenant now lying in a pool of blood, Horne snatched the knife from Babcock and, with one deft slice, broke his rule about not taking human lives.

26

The Town Major

THE GOVERNOR'S HOUSE

Horne and Babcock emerged from the gate fronting the Guardhouse as a cockerel's crow carried into the fortress from the Black Town. They each grabbed a bale of straw from the line in front of the building and, hoisting the bales to their shoulders, made their way diagonally across the Parade towards the bastion on the southwest corner of the stone wall surrounding the Governor's House.

As they passed along the south side of the wall, Kiro emerged from the shadows of the six white columns of the English Church and fell into step beside them.

Walking three abreast, the men turned left at the southeast corner of the Governor's House and walked north along St. Thomas Street, passing the locked entrance to the Governor's House on their left, the stately procession of stone columns stretching down towards the Sea Gate to their right.

Groot appeared from the shadows at the northeast corner of the thick wall which formed the inner fortress.

Horne stopped. He shifted the straw bale from one shoulder to the other and glanced back down St. Thomas Street. St. Thomas Gate was still closed. Were Jingee and Jud nearby? The six o'clock bells would start ringing soon.

Babcock, Kiro, and Groot stood facing Horne. Groot noticed the bruises on Horne's face but did not ask questions. Standing with his back to Portuguese Square, he reported, "They've taken General Lally to the Portuguese Church, *schupper*."

"How heavy's the guard?" Horne looked beyond Groot's shoulder at the spire of the small church.

"Two guards in front. Four behind. You can't see the front guards, *schupper*, because they're standing by the doors."

"What about inside the church?"

"I counted six men go in, *schupper*, and four come out."

Horne remembered the details about the Portuguese Church. "Were you able to see if they're still working on the church?"

"I looked through a side window. I saw boards piled on the floor. Stones and mortar all around in heaps."

Stepping closer to Horne, Groot added in a lower voice, "I was also able to listen, *schupper*. I heard a Lieutenant say he must report to the Town Major. It's the same Lieutenant whom Babcock and I saw at the

Barracks. His name's Mason, He's gone down there now—" Groot nodded behind Horne, "—to the Town Hall. You just missed running into him."

Horne glanced back down the street. The Town Major's office was in the Town Hall, halfway down St. Thomas Street, situated between the spot where they were standing and St. Thomas Gate. Were the Town Major and the Lieutenant in there now making changes? Planning to move Lally a second time? Why? What was happening? Did someone suspect a plot?

Horne thought of the original plan he had made with his seven men. "Jud and Jingee should be at St. Thomas Gate by now. Bapu and Mustafa, in the Stables. We're already running short of time so we can't make too many changes."

He looked at Kiro. "You and I will go to the Portuguese Church."

Kiro nodded.

To Babcock, he said, "Give Kiro your bale."

Babcock hoisted the straw onto Kiro's back.

Horne looked at Groot. "You keep to the same plan. Go to the Stables. But instead of getting two extra horses, bring a third one. For Kiro. Bring the horses to the gate in front of the Portuguese Church. Across the square from the Magazine. Leave the Stables when the bells start ringing at six o'clock. Understand?"

"Aye, aye, *schupper.*"

Horne looked back at Babcock. "You keep to the same plan too, Babcock."

Babcock patted the leather pouch hanging from his belt.

Horne stood facing the small half-circle of men.

"When we come out of the church, we ride down this side of the Governor's House. Turn here. Head down St. Thomas Street. If we see that Jud and Jingee haven't got the gates open, we chance leaving through the Sea Gate."

Resettling the bale on his shoulder, he said, "Kiro, I'll explain our plan of action on the way to the church."

"Yes, sir."

Horne looked from Kiro to Groot to Babcock. "This is it."

THE TOWN HALL

The Town Major had seen them. Alexander Shipton, Town Major, Chief Deputy to Governor Pigot, and Company Officer-in-Command during Pigot's absence, had watched two men with bales on their shoulders walk down the south wall of the Governor's House. A third man joined them from the English Church as they continued down to St. Thomas Street. Where were workmen going so early in the morning? Why had a man come out of the English Church? Wasn't it locked? Or was reconstruction work being done there— as inside the Portuguese Church—that he didn't know about?

Shipton had been unable to sleep this morning. He had been troubled by all the problems which had risen in Pigot's absence. Having come early to work in his office, his presence in the Town Hall had proved to be well-timed—Lieutenant Mason had come here reporting that General Lally was being moved to a new prison.

Waiting for Mason to report back on Lally's whereabouts, Shipton had stood at the window, reading the letter which had created all the problems.

> *I have the pleasure to acquaint you that the Garrison of Pondicherry surrendered themselves on Discretion on the 16th instant. In the morning of the same day we took possession of the Veillenour Gate and in the evening of the Citadel. I beg leave to congratulate you of this happy event. Eyre Coote. 19th January. 1761.*

A knock sounded on the door as Shipton stood at the window, holding the letter and looking down at the two workmen turning the corner of St. Thomas Street with the bales of straw on their shoulders. Shipton moved towards his desk, calling for the early morning visitor to enter.

Lieutenant Mason stepped into Shipton's office, his craggy cheeks flushed with excitement. Approaching the desk, he saluted, reporting, "Sir, General Lally's been moved to the Portuguese Church."

"The Portuguese Church?" Shipton sank back into his chair. "Why there of all places?"

"Lally's Roman Catholic, sir. His confessor, Father Lavour, used to say Mass at the Portuguese Church and he feels safe there."

Shipton frowned. "How large is the guard?"

"Eight, sir."

"Double—no, treble it. Immediately."

"There's also another matter to report, sir. Two men have been found dead in the Guardhouse. Killed in the room where General Lally had been imprisoned."

"Killed?" Shipton stared disbelievingly at Mason.

"Yes, sir. Captain Oliver Giltspur and Lieutenant Abel Edwards. Both of the 64th, sir."

"For any apparent reason, Lieutenant?"

"No, sir. There was no one else on that floor. No sign of entry. It obviously happened only shortly after General Lally had been moved."

Shipton took a deep breath, looking at Eyre Coote's letter about Pondicherry's surrender lying on his desk. "Perhaps Lally wasn't talking nonsense about assassins."

"I'm beginning to think the same, sir."

Shipton raised his eyes. "Mason, I'm taking personal command of this situation. I'll return with you to the Portuguese Church."

ST. THOMAS GATE

Two hundred and fifty yards south of the Town Hall, Jingee moved from the shadows of the narrow alleyway leading from St. Thomas Bastion to St. Thomas Gate. Carrying two steaming tin mugs and a covered tray, he sat cross-legged on the cobblestones in front of the empty guard kiosk. A few minutes passed before two uniformed guards for the morning's first sentry duty came down the alleyway. They slowed when they saw Jingee waiting for them, expressions of curiosity on their faces, smiles of pleasure cracking when they spied the two steaming mugs and covered breakfast tray. Jud stepped behind the guards in the alley, crooking his strong black arm around one man's neck. Jingee pulled a cudgel from the tray and attacked the second guard.

27

The English Bells

THE PORTUGUESE CHURCH

The Portuguese Church was little larger than a chapel. Built in the sixteenth century by Portuguese traders from Lisbon, the ornate red brick and white stucco church was anachronistic in company with the later, simpler stone structures erected by the East India Company.

Adam Horne and Kiro, bent under the weight of the straw bales on their backs, passed through the wrought iron gates fronting the flag walk. They moved down a short avenue of palm trees towards two guards standing by the carved cedar doors opening into the vestibule.

Keeping his head low as he approached the left guard, Horne used the officer's name Groot had told him. "Lieutenant mason wants these."

The guard looked quizzical. "Straw? What does he want straw for?"

"For . . . *this*!"

Horne charged forward with the bale, pushing the man back into the vestibule; Kiro moved at the same time, butting the second guard towards the marble floor.

Slamming shut the doors, Horne pulled the iron bar. He spun around, bringing down his boot on the first guard's musket barrel as he chopped him behind the neck, kneeing him on the chin.

Kiro attacked the second guard, sending his musket to the floor and, facing him with both hands raised, palms open, he levelled his left hand in a sharp *karate* strike and followed with a hit from the other hand.

Horne and Kiro striped off the guards' jackets, gagged them, bound their hands and feet, and tied them back-to-back on the vestibule floor. Hurriedly dressing in the jackets, they moved into the nave. Groot's information had been correct; the church had been stripped to bare brick, and piles of lumber and stone were heaped across the flagging.

Horne knocked on the door at the rear of the nave. "Mason here."

A bolt shot back on the far side of the door.

Pushing open the door, Horne jabbed his knife at the man unlocking it, a squat Sergeant with a bushy red moustache.

Kiro slipped past the Sergeant into the sacristy, grabbing the barrel of the other guard's musket. Swinging the butt at his face, he knocked him to the floor.

Horne held his knife to the Sergeant's throat. "Where's Lally?"

The Sergeant's small green eyes darted to a door

decorated with a cross. Looking back to Horne and Kiro, he tried to compose himself but his voice still wavered as he said, "I don't know who you are . . . But there's men outside . . . You better not kill us because . . ."

Horne pulled back his left hand, sending the Sergeant to the floor with a *Pankration* chop. Kiro used a *Karate* blow on the other guard.

After binding and gagging both men, Horne moved to the left of the door marked with the cross. He knocked twice and paused before knocking a third time.

A voice immediately answered. "Who is it?"

"General Lally?"

"Who is it?" repeated the voice.

Horne knocked again and, keeping his voice low, asked, "Do you know Father Lavour? *Père* Lavour?"

The door flew open. A white-haired man stood facing Horne.

Jabbing the knife towards Lally's throat, Horne ordered, "Open your mouth, General, and you'll be buried in this church."

Lally's blue eyes were bloodshot with fatigue. He stared at Horne's bruised face, at the Regimental jacket he was wearing, then at the two bound guards on the floor.

Looking from Horne to Kiro, he asked, "Who are you?"

"Your escorts, sir." Horne motioned him out of the room with the knife.

Lally showed none of the guards' fears. "Where are you taking me? What's the reason for this?"

"You'll find out soon enough." Horne pulled a kerchief from his breeches.

Lally demanded, "Did the French send you, damn it? D'Ache? Rambeau? What's the reason for—"

The kerchief muffled the rest of Lally's words. Horne bound his hands in front of him with leather thongs as Kiro primed the guards' brace of flintlocks.

Cautiously but firmly, Horne pushed Lally from the sacristy, moving him across the nave, Kiro followed, keeping his back to them, holding both pistols trained on the rear door.

They reached the vestibule as the six o'clock bells began ringing across the fortress from the English Church.

THE STABLES

At the sound of the six o'clock bells, Bapu stepped from the Stables. Still dressed in a turban and *dhoti*, he looked across the Parade towards the top of Portuguese Square. All was clear.

Beckoning towards the darkness of the Stables, Bapu stepped back against the door as Groot and Babcock clattered forward on their mounts.

Groot, leading three horses behind him, moved across the Parade at a neat trot as Babcock followed more slowly on his roan.

Watching the two men turn from the Parade into Portuguese Square, Bapu disappeared back into the Stables. He emerged a few seconds later riding a chestnut mare and gripping the reins of a black stallion and a sturdy grey mare. Mustafa rode alongside him on a dappled mare as they cantered along the south side of the Governor's House, down towards St. Thomas Street, passing the English Church where the bells still rang noisily in the new day.

THE MAGAZINE

Babcock reached the opposite side of the Governor's House from Bapu and Mustafa and reined his roan by the Magazine built into the sloping northwest corner of the thick yellow stone wall.

Listening to the bells pealing, he pulled a flint light and a parchment of explosives from his leather pouch as he watched Groot lead the three horses down Portuguese Square.

The sound of running feet came from the front of the church, and Babcock saw Horne and Kiro burst through the gate with a gagged white-haired man—Lally!

Babcock struck the flint.

He watched Horne shove Lally astride the black stallion and mount the saddle behind him, then he lit the fuse and lobbed the explosives towards the Magazine's grille.

ST. THOMAS STREET

Town Major Shipton, accompanied by Lieutenant Mason, closed the front door of the Town Hall as the six o'clock bells finished pealing. They were on their way to the Portuguese Church.

Stepping from the porch, they heard the rumble of

galloping horses and looked to their left down St. Thomas Street.

Three horses raced between the open gates. Shipton and Mason saw four more riders in the distance, dust rising behind them as they galloped towards the beach in the early morning light.

At the sound of another horse, Shipton and Mason turned and saw a man galloping towards them on a roan. Lieutenant Mason pulled his sabre to stop him. But a loud explosion shook the earth and the horse thundered past them.

28

The Wild Geese

Adam Horne disliked running a horse to his limits, especially in the heat of the day. But not knowing if the cloud of dust behind him rose from somebody in pursuit, he kept pushing the stallion, continuing south across the Carnatic Plain towards the Chingleput Hills. Having untied Lally's mouth gag he continued riding behind him, removing all temptation for Lally to attack him.

By mid-morning, the cloud of dust had disappeared in the north. Horne guessed that the rider had been Babcock—the last man to leave Fort St. George—and that he had switched to an inland route.

Chancing a rest stop on a sandstone ridge protected by a blind of yellowing cedars, Horne dismounted and slit the leather thongs from Lally's wrist. In silence they shared the waterskin which Bapu had tied to the saddle.

Thereafter they stopped at regular intervals. Horne

guessed that the time was midday when he halted at the mouth of a shallow valley dotted with milk grass. Seeing no dust clouds to the north, he hoped that Babcock's explosion in the Magazine had successfully diverted attention in the fortress from the fact that Lally was missing.

Two hours had passed since the escape. So far Lally had not spoken to Horne. His temper was legendary and Horne was surprised that he had not tried to deliver at least a harangue to him.

When Lally did finally speak, he didn't look at Horne. His voice touched with contempt, he said, "You're not in the British Army, are you?"

Horne lowered the waterskin and eyed Lally, wary about answering any questions.

Tall and thick-chested, Lally looked distinguished despite the dust caking his face and the kerchief tied haphazardly over his head to protect him from the sun.

Lally turned his eyes to Horne. "Who are you? Where are you taking me?"

"Your questions will all be answered in due course."

Lally held his nose aloft. "You're not in the British Army or the Navy but neither are you an agent for France."

Horne stopped the waterskin. "We must make time."

Knotting the skin bag to the saddle, Horne gestured for General Lally to remount in front of him.

Continuing south over the parched, barren countryside, the horse tired more quickly in the afternoon heat. Horne rested the animal at shorter intervals and, by the time the sun began descending from its zenith, he was pleased with their progress. They had passed Sharuna's murky blue reservoir at least an hour ago and should be arriving at their rendezvous with the *Eclipse* before sundown.

Certain that nobody was following them, Horne now looked for dust in front of them, some sign of the seven other horses. Seeing nothing, he reminded himself that the men had spread out across inland trails and were all riding solitary. A single mount made better time than two men astride the same horse.

Lally's white shirt had become brown from dust, the kerchief soggy with perspiration. Complaining neither about the heat nor the dried meat and biscuits which Bapu had packed for sustenance, the General had neither attacked nor berated Horne. He seemed almost content as they rested on a precipice over the Bay of Bengal, a cool breeze sweeping inland from a cloud-streaked sky.

"Did you fight with Wolfe in Canada?"

The question surprised Horne. "Why?"

Lally filled his lungs with fresh air as he stared out at the blue expanse. "Warfare is changing. Men are more concerned these days with survival than chivalry. Brute endurance. We learn these things from the colonies. Orientals teach us their wily ways. We glean lessons in camouflage and tracking and ambush from those Canadian savages, redskins, so wrongly called—" he laughed, "—Indians."

Lally's English was untouched by Irish brogue or French accent. Speaking in a deep, resonant voice, he talked to Horne like a man speaking to—if not his peer—someone who could quite possibly understand him.

Gazing out at the eastern horizon, he announced, "I've been studying you. You don't have the ways of so-called 'gentleman' officers. That's why I asked you about serving under Wolfe in Canada."

The statement piqued Horne.

Lally held his gaze towards the sea, the blue mirrored by the pale colour of his eyes. "You obviously know who I am or you wouldn't be going to all this trouble. You must therefore know something about my history. That I commanded many mercenaries in my day. I say this because you're closer to a mercenary than any other soldier I know."

Horne remained cautious, remembering that conversation with prisoners was dangerous, especially when a man was as crafty as Lally was reputed to be.

"You've heard of the Wild Geese, haven't you? The Irish mercenaries I led?"

"Since I was a schoolboy."

Lally turned to study Horne, looking more closely at him as if for the first time he realised that he was a very young man. "Who are you?"

Horne felt a sudden urge to talk and listen to Lally. To hear about the Wild Geese. To tell him about Elihu Cornhill, the man who had taught him the ways of North American Indians—scouting, camouflage, the use of daybreak as a time for attack.

But remembering that he had allowed his personal impulses to overcome him once already today, Horne stood back for Lally to remount the horse. "We must keep riding"—he added, "—sir."

Lally gripped the saddle but hesitated. Looking at Horne, he asked, "You believe I had no choice but to surrender, don't you? My men were without food, water. Morale was non-existent. Surrender was the only choice I had."

Horne felt the same urge to confide, to tell Lally about a thought nagging him, that he had not intended to waste human life on this mission. But Oliver Giltspur had joked about the only person he had ever loved and he had had no choice but to kill him.

Holding out his hand towards the horse, Horne repeated, "Sir, we must keep riding."

Approaching the rendezvous inlet on the Chingleput coast, Horne slowed the stallion as he spotted the masts of Commodore Watson's flagship, the *Ferocious*, at anchor in the lagoon beyond the stone escarpment. Why had the *Eclipse* not come as they had planned? And where was *La Favourite*? Had Watson left both ships at sea? Or had the *Eclipse* sailed to Bengal as an escort for the French prize?

Dismounting at the summit, Horne saw a rowing boat moving out from the sandy white shore, rowing around the tip of the rocky point of the escarpment towards the *Ferocious*. He was too far away to count the number of men in the small boat. But they spotted him and their cheer carried up the hill.

Returning the wave, Horne checked his feeling of victory. He must first learn if all seven men had come back from Fort St. George—that no one had been injured in the escape—before he began to celebrate.

Keeping Lally in the saddle, he led the stallion down

the incline to the beach, where Tim Flannery was carrying supplies from the hut.

Flannery turned at the sound of the horse's nicker.

The heels of Horne's boots sank in the sand. "Have all the men returned, Mr. Flannery?"

Flannery looked from Horne to Lally sitting silently astride the big stallion. Holding his watery green eyes on Lally, Flannery answered, "Aye, they've been straggling back all afternoon."

Helping Lally dismount, Horne ordered, "Mr. Flannery, give this gentleman a place to rest whilst I unsaddle the horse. The boat will return to collect us soon."

The sweet aroma of liquor wafted from Flannery as he led Lally across the beach towards the hut, and Horne was thankful that the General needed no medical attention.

The stallion had lathered in the heat. Horne unsaddled the animal, patting the beast's great neck, pleased to be setting him free with the seven other horses grazing peacefully on small clumps of brown grass. They could roam the nearby hills until some lucky farmer claimed them, hopefully giving them a good home.

Thinking about the future, Horne looked back to the *Ferocious*, wondering where Watson would take Lally from here? Deliver him to the ship sailing for England? What would Lally's future be in England? Would the British use him as a pawn in their colonial battles? Or would the war soon come to an end?

A shot shattered the stillness.

•   •   •

The rowing boat's six oars cut the rippling water in a neat dry row, moving from the shore to the *Ferocious*. Lally sat ashen-faced between the fore oarsmen, one hand clutching a bloody cloth to his left shoulder where Flannery's bullet had grazed him. In the stern of the boat Flannery sat cursing Horne for preventing him from getting his revenge.

"Lally sent my brother into the firing line at Fontenoy," he raged. "Those lads had no hope that day against the English cannons. But Lally drove them on and on and on. Straight into Cumberland's volley. I heard the story from one of the few survivors. That was sixteen years ago and I swore then that I'd kill this devil for sending my brother to slaughter. And I'll kill you too, Horne, for stopping me."

Horne stood in the prow of the open boat, waiting to catch the rope ladder dangling from the *Ferocious*. He was at least thankful that Flannery had been too drunk to hit his target.

From the stern, Flannery ranted, "Horne, you're no better than Lally. Your seven sea rats mean no more to you than Lally's Wild Geese did to him. You both use innocent lads to serve your own glory. May you both swing at the end of a rope."

The oars stilled as the boat moved alongside the *Ferocious*. Horne grabbed the ladder, standing back for Lally to try and grasp the rungs.

The shot from Flannery's flintlock had only grazed Lally's shoulder and he was able to climb the hemp ladder. Two of the flagship's Marines waited at the port entry to lead him across deck.

Horne motioned Flannery to climb next from the rowing boat.

Pausing in front of Horne, Flannery cursed, "May you roam the world for the rest of your days. May you starve to death—"

The oarsmen behind Flannery shoved him towards the ladder. Grabbing it, Flannery spat in Horne's face and began to climb upwards. The oarsmen reached to pull Flannery from the ladder, but Horne touched his shoulder and shook his head as he wiped the spittle from his face.

Horne boarded the flagship. He was pleased to find Watson waiting to welcome him at the port entry, but surprised to see him looking so old and weary.

Gripping Horne's hands, Watson rasped, "Today should be the proudest day of your life, Horne. Let's be done with the bad news so that we can move on to congratulations."

Bad news? Horne did not understand.

Watson put his hand on Horne's shoulder. "We lost the *Eclipse*."

Horne stiffened.

His arm around Horne, Watson explained, "Frenchie caught us the afternoon we left you in this very bay."

"Frenchie"? Horne's mind flashed back to the English frigate which had stopped the *masulah* that night, to the English lieutenant who had told Jingee about French ships being sighted off the coast of Attur.

"Horne, your men fought a good battle. Young Mercer and Bruce proved to be true heroes. Tandimmer was a master sailor. And game ankle or no, Rajit died a credit to the Bombay Marine."

Horne realised what Watson was saying. All the men had been lost. He gazed at him, seeking confirmation.

Watson shook his head. "Not one survivor."

Horne glanced over Watson's shoulder at the line of seven Marines waiting for him. "Do my other men know?"

"I told them." Watson patted Horne's shoulder. "Go and rest. My cabin is yours. We'll discuss this later."

Horne felt numb. "Thank you, sir, but I still have my duty."

"Duty? Duty be hanged? Go and rest. You need it!"

"Thank you, sir, but I must speak to my men."

Not waiting for Watson's consent, Horne moved towards the seven men waiting in the waist of the ship.

Caked with dust, soaked with perspiration, the seven men looked anxiously at Horne moving towards them from the port entry.

Bapu still wore the turban and *dhoti*, his skin filthy from riding through the Indian countryside; Kiro's face was masked with dirt, only his white teeth and dark oriental eyes gleaming beneath the grime; Mustafa smiled broadly through his coating of dust—the first smile Horne had seen cross his face; Jud's smile was familiar and friendly, seeming as big as Africa itself; Groot beamed with a lift of his eyebrows; Jingee bowed from the waist delivering a courtly *salaam*; Babcock snapped a mock salute but quickly relaxed, grinning as he pulled one of his ears.

Horne stood in front of the seven men, his eyes moving down the line of dirty, oddly matched faces. "We should be celebrating, but that's impossible with the bad news that was waiting for us."

His voice had become faint, his sunburnt face beginning to show lines of fatigue. "I don't want to keep you from eating or getting some rest. I just want to thank you for doing a fine job. For proving to the Company that you're the men I knew you were—or that I knew you wanted to be."

He paused, considering a thought, then took a deep breath and continued, "I should also say that you've helped me become more of the man *I* want to be. You showed me that a man should have friends. Thank you for that too."

Glancing one last time at the line of seven dirty faces, Horne saluted and turned towards the companionway. A loud cheer rose behind him.

Afterword

It is historical fact that Thomas Lally´ was delivered to England aboard a merchant ship, the *Onslow*, in April, 1761. The British War Office allowed him to return to France a few months later to clear his name of "Treason, incompetence, correspondence with the English, speculation, and tyrannical administration." The French imprisoned Lally in the Bastille, stripped him of his fortune, rank and title, and guillotined him in 1766. A detailed sketch of Lally's life is available in the remarkably helpful book, *Men Whom India Has Known* by J. J. Higginbotham, Madras, 1874. Another unique and valuable source for this period is *Vestiges of Old Madras 1640–1800* by Henry Love, John Murray, 1913. There are countless memoirs, sketches, gazeteers available on India, the East India Company, and the Seven Years War. But information is scant on history's earliest commando-style squadron, the Bombay Marine. The best source is Low's *History of the Indian*

Navy, London, 1877. Except for Commodore James and Commodore Watson, the names and characters of the Bombay Marines I portray are fictitious. The story is based on fact with fictional elaboration and twists which will become apparent to those readers who wish to delve deeper into this rich, adventurous period of Indian history.

—Porter Hill

Glossary

Bhang—a marijuana beverage

Bilboes—shipboard shackles devised in the Spanish foundries of Bilbao

Brahmin—the highest Hindu caste

Castas—the Portuguese word for Hindu system of castes

Compagnie des Indes Orientales—The French East India Company

Dharma—Hindu intrinsic duty of life

Dhoolie—a covered litter

Dhoti—loincloth

Dongi—small canoe made from leaves

Dubash—literally, 'two languages,' hence an interpreter or secretary

Dungri—coarse blue Indian cotton weave, the original 'dungarees' or blue 'jeans'

Hookah—waterpipe for smoking tobacco or marijuana

Feringhi—foreigner

Kshatriya——the second highest and Hindu warrior caste

Masulah—the sewn plank boats used in the Madras surf

Nautch—low women, prostitutes

Pahar—division of Indian time

Pankration—ancient manner of Greek combat, forerunner of Japanese Karate

Panchama—literally, 'the fifth,' people outside the four Indian castes

Pisces—small India copper currency

Punkah—overhead fan operated by rope

Raga—Indian music form

"Ram"—Hindu war chant to the god, Rama

Rasa—mood or feeling

Sari—female garb, long cloth

Sepoy—Indian troop trained by European standards

Sudra—people below the Hindu high castes

Tilaki—cosmetic dot worn on Indian women's foreheads

Topiwallah—literally, men with hats; hence, foreigners

Ulank—a harbour boat or barge

Vaisya—the third Hindu caste, the powerful merchant class